BILLIONAIRE'S BALLET

A Standalone Prequel to the Lovers Dance Series

---

by Deanna Roy

Six-Time *USA Today* bestselling author of
The Forever Series
The Lovers Dance Series

I0685193

Casey Shay Press
PO Box 160116
Austin, TX 78716
www.caseyshaypress.com

E-ISBN: 9781938150586

Also available in paperback as Billionaire's Ballet:
ISBN: 9781938150593
Library of Congress Control Number: 2016908824

eBook version 3.0

Summary

A woman must choose between the wealthy man she has loved since childhood...and his brother.

Get emails or texts from Deanna about her new releases:
Deanna's List

For Janice Roy
January 1953 - May 2016

My Mom
My Biggest Fan
Sorry I didn't finish this one quite in time.
I know how much you loved Sabrina.
(Although I'm sure you'll figure out a way to read it anyway.)

Foreword

Author's Note:

I first saw the Audrey Hepburn movie *Sabrina* as an impressionable young girl. Having grown up in a tiny town and feeling incredibly naive and unsophisticated, I loved the idea that maybe I, too, could go away for a few years and return to be the belle of the ball..

(Spoiler alert: it didn't work.)

While the tale of Quinn, Bennett, and Juliet's love triangle is from my own heart and imagination, I hope you will spot a few homages to the film in this story.

Chapter One

❧

San Antonio, Texas
August 2010

WHEN THEY WROTE THAT SONG ABOUT THE STARS being big and bright in Texas, they were definitely talking about a night like this.

The rough edge of limestone scraped my shins as I moved along the garden wall to get a better look at the party. Above me, the summer sky was clear and bursting with stars. The Big Dipper stood out, ready to serve up something cool and refreshing from the water below.

The night was hot enough that I longed to take a dip myself. The cascading swimming pools at the back of the Claremont estate sparkled like a reflection of the sky. Magnolias as big as dinner plates floated on the surface. And around the edges, women in shimmery dresses and men in Texas tuxedos of blue jeans and suit jackets held each other close as they danced.

I hung on to the ledge as I scanned the crowd for the face I wanted to see. It might be the last time I got to look at him before I left town tomorrow. And I wanted to take a big long drink of his presence, something to hold me over in the lonely nights in New York, where I didn't know a soul.

The double French doors at the back of the house opened wide, like someone wanted to make an entrance. I knew who it would be. Of course.

Quinn.

My breath caught when I saw him. His unruly hair looked like someone had just raked their fingers through it. His jaw was scruffy and hard-edged. Even from this distance, I could see the mischief in his hazel eyes.

The party seemed to pause and take a breath with his appearance. The band finished the slow song and counted into a number with a lot more pep. The laughter seemed brighter and the noise level kicked up a notch as people greeted him.

Quinn had that effect on everything. Parties. Women. Definitely me.

I had known him all my life.

He was three years old when I was born in one of the guest cottages on this estate. My mom was the family's full-time dance instructor.

I'd seen each expression he'd made since. I could close my eyes and picture every single one.

Quinn, eyes dancing as he sprinted ahead of me across the lawns. His laughter as we rode horses on the back trail. His happy eagerness as we jumped off a stack of bales in the barn into a pile of loose hay. When we were young, our friendship had been easy and fun.

He had even kissed me once, on my tenth birthday. His father had bought a new horse for the stable, a blue-gray mare for me to ride. She wasn't quite broken for riding, but in my excitement, I saddled her anyway.

We didn't make it four steps before she bucked, and I landed on my rear end in the dust.

Quinn rushed out to the ring and lifted me up. I had tears in my eyes and he'd kissed my lids, first one, then the other.

I'm pretty sure that's the moment it happened.

I fell in love.

He'd been my obsession. The boy no one else could ever measure up to.

Not that I'd ever let anybody try.

Down at the party, Quinn draped his arms across the shoulders of the Monroe twins. My tender heart sank a bit more. He'd never put his arm around me like that. I'd never gotten to wear something slinky and grown-up around him. Despite my debilitating crush, I worked hard to stay a friend and confidant even as he went to college and slid into the role of playboy billionaire.

Now I was eighteen and he was twenty-one. And worlds apart in every way.

So it was just as well I was leaving for New York.

A voice called from down below. "Juliet?"

Shoot, my mother. I lay as flat as possible on the top of the wall. It was close to eight feet high. Maybe she wouldn't see me up here.

Mom wandered up the path from our little guest-house toward the main estate. She walked with the grace of a longtime dancer, each foot placed daintily in front of the other. Her flowing skirt fluttered around her knees. The lights shined on her black hair, the same inky gloss as mine.

She had raised me to be a dancer as soon as I could walk. And I had worked hard to be as good as she wanted me to be.

But I wasn't positive I had the talent or the drive to do the one thing she always wished for herself — a spot at a prestigious ballet company.

Tomorrow morning, I would find out. She'd take me to the airport and send me to a dance school in one of the most exciting cities in the world. There I would learn what I was made of. I had never been trained by anyone but her.

All I could do was try.

Mother hadn't spotted me yet, so I turned back to the party.

Quinn had deserted the twins and was dancing with a girl I didn't recognize. She was lovely, pale and blond, tall and willowy. She couldn't dance, though. Every so often they had to pause because she lost her footing.

After a few more missteps, Quinn pulled her close and they moved together in a slow shuffle, her cheek on his chest.

I had to look away.

"I see you up there, Juliet," Mom said. "Are you spying on another party?" She stood at the base of the wall and peered up in disapproval. "I'm sure you only had to have asked and the girls would have invited you."

I knew who she meant by "the girls" and frowned at the mention of the Claremont sisters. I searched the party and spotted Rose and Pearl. They were hiding in a dark corner, both too young to really join the festivities. Rose was thirteen and snobby to the core. Pearl was only ten, but looked up to her sister and followed her lead.

Neither were talented dancers, but Mom always worked with what she got. Dance had been a critical component of the Claremont lifestyle, and my mother had been hired at the birth of Estelle, the eldest Claremont, and kept on full-time.

Fortunately the Claremonts had more girls, so Mother had a job here at least until Pearl grew up. By then, hopefully I would be situated somewhere that I could bring her with me.

Where was Quinn? I'd lost him in the crowd.

I had only just found him again among the party-goers' when I felt my mother tug on my ankle. I looked back. She had climbed up behind me.

"It's our last night," she said softly. "I had hoped to spend a little time together."

She was right. Watching Quinn flirt with girls at his social level wasn't going to make my final moments on the estate any better.

I swung my legs around and jumped down. Mom followed with a graceful leap and put her arm around my waist. I fell in beside her and our steps naturally moved at the same gait. She had taught me well, and now was my time to shine. I had to buck up, put my past behind me, and get over Quinn.

Chapter Two

❧

My evening with Mom had been cozy and calm, going through my bags and making sure my accounts and credit cards were in order.

But there was no way I could sleep.

I opened my window. The sounds of the party still filtered past the wall. It was winding down. I knew these events well. When they began, glasses clinked, greetings were shouted, and the music swelled.

The party would crescendo like a dramatic moment in an opera. The voices would become a wave of sound. Laughter would break out. Inevitably something would get broken or crash.

Then cars would begin to leave, one by one. The casual attendees moved on, and the smaller group of those who had settled in would remain until the wee hours. That's where things were now.

I heard a splash and some laughter. Someone was in the pool. I pictured Quinn skinny-dipping with the blond and my throat felt thick.

He had no idea I felt this way. I had never let it show. But I couldn't stay away, not this night, my last one. Maybe if I told him how I felt, it would change things.

Yes, maybe he was hiding it too! And I would explain it to him, and he would smile and say, "If only I had known!" And "Of course you can't go to New York! You must stay."

And he would kiss me. Not on my eyelids, but a real honest-to-goodness kiss on the mouth.

The feel of soft grass on my bare feet surprised me. I looked behind and realized I was out the window.

I should go back. Get my rest. Prepare for the early morning and the flight.

But I didn't.

A line of small Malibu lights illuminated the path, but I kept away from their glow. The shrubs and trees hid me as I moved toward the main estate. I couldn't see over the stone wall without climbing it again, but my tiny white sleep shorts and spaghetti-strap shirt might make me visible against the night sky.

God, I was walking out here in my pajamas!

I felt bold. Something hot bolted through me as I

imagined Quinn seeing me in this outfit. I glanced down at the thin stretchy shirt. No bra. That was obvious. I shivered.

I walked along the wall until I came to a gate. I peeked through the iron bars. A few people sat around the pool, dipping their legs in. A girl in a bra and panties was in the water splashing around.

But Quinn wasn't part of the group.

His older brother Bennett stood alone near the door of the house, drinking something from a short glass. His face shifted my way and I jumped behind the stone wall, praying he hadn't seen me. He was the type to investigate if he thought something was awry.

When I looked again, though, he had turned to go inside.

He paused to talk to someone just beyond the outer door, then moved aside. It was Quinn! The brothers nodded at each other, and Quinn headed out to the patio. He was holding a bottle of wine and two glasses. A white towel was draped over his arm.

No! Surely not the girl in the pool.

But he only tossed a towel to her. I let out a long breath. The blond girl was still there in her shimmery dress. She smiled shyly as he handed her a glass.

They walked toward the back gate, the one that led to the barn. I couldn't help myself, but hurried along the wall until I reached the corner.

I peeked around. Quinn and the girl were moving toward the stables. My heart clenched.

Quinn often took girls back to the horse barn. I had heard him joke about "a roll in the hay." This was not something I ever spied on, but tonight was different. I felt pulled by an invisible force.

The two of them were oblivious to me. I sprinted from tree to tree, keeping to the shadows. Quinn opened the door and stepped aside to let the girl enter ahead of him.

I rushed to the opposite side of the barn where the feed was loaded in. After a quick fumble with the combination lock, I ducked inside, feeling my way in the dark.

I knew it well, having come to visit my blue mare Jezebelle often these eight years since that fateful birthday. I stuck my hand in the grain bag and grasped a fistful, my alibi if I should be caught. Saying good-bye to my horse the night before I left might seem sentimental and silly, but it would make sense.

Laughter in the main corridor between the stalls made me pause. I cracked the door to the feed room and watched Quinn set the wine and glasses on a shelf. He took the girl in his arms.

The barn was clean and the floor smooth. A single lamp high on the wall was the only dim light.

They danced together a moment in the silence,

the girl still awkward, but game to try. I closed my eyes as he leaned in for a kiss. I imagined it were me there instead.

When I opened them again, the girl was pulling away. "Too much wine already," she said with a small laugh. "Nature calls."

Quinn pointed down the corridor to the bathroom, just past a little break room where the horse trainers always had lunch.

I leaned farther to watch her go, trying to figure out if she was tipsy. But the door was cracked too much and flew open, dumping me unceremoniously out onto the floor.

Quinn whirled around. "What the hell?" Then he saw me and hurried forward. "Jules! Are you all right?"

My face burned hot as he knelt on one knee in front of me. He smelled like pine woods and dark beer. He held out a hand to help me up.

I took it and realized too late it still had bits of grain stuck to it. Even so, he smiled and brought me to my feet. When he let go, he brushed his palm against his jeans. "Saying good-bye to Jezebelle?" he asked.

I nodded, struck mute by my proximity to him while I was wearing so little.

"You okay?" Quinn asked. He punched me lightly

on the arm. "Did you sneak some of the party liquor?"

I struggled to keep myself together. Despite my age, he viewed me as a kid. He had grown up, but I was still ten to him. The three years between us were huge now. And I was leaving home to become my own person. I had been foolish to think our situation could ever be any other way.

"Cat got your tongue?" he asked.

"No," I said, shaking my head. "It's just a big night."

"I'll say," Quinn said. "You should have come to the party. Made it a going-away thing."

I wanted to chide him for saying that now, when it was too late, but then he had never thought of things like that. He seemed oblivious to how my birthdays were always held out in the guesthouse or on the pavilion out by the tank. Never inside the walls of the estate.

He glanced behind me, and I wondered if the girl was back. But she must not have been, because he opened the door to the feed room and grasped his own handful of grain. "Let's go tell the old girl good-bye," he said.

We walked along the stalls until we came to the one at the end. Quinn opened the top half of the door. Jezebelle shuffled forward, her ears pricked.

"Hello, girl," Quinn said. "Up for a midnight snack? Last one from your lady."

He lifted my hand and my heart stuttered. His mischievous eyes met mine for a moment, and everything I'd ever loved about him blasted at me with the power of a freight train.

I imagined him pressing a kiss to my palm, and my breath froze in my chest.

But he only poured half the grain into my hand. Then he held his out to the horse. "Here you go, old girl," he said. "I'll come and let you know how Jules is doing." He glanced back at me with another twinkle of his eyes. "As long as she stays in touch."

"Of course I will," I said, trying to force the tremble out of my voice. I held out my hand. Jezebelle's warm mouth nuzzled into my palm. My chest tightened. I was leaving her too. Everybody and everything I loved. I could barely stand it.

Footsteps came down the corridor. We turned to the blond girl, who looked startled to see me. Her eyes glanced at my outfit and then rested questioningly on Quinn.

"Daughter of one of the staff," he said. "Has lived here since she was born, right, Jules?"

I nodded.

The girl seemed mollified. "You had some wine for me?" she asked.

Quinn backed away from the stall, brushing his hands together. "That I do." He gave me a little pat on the head, like I was four. "Good luck tomorrow, Jules. You'll do great in the Big Apple."

They headed off down the hall, pausing only to pick up the wine and glasses from the shelf. I turned back to Jezebelle, flooded with despair. It wasn't right. I'd known Quinn forever. How could I leave him?

Fat tears rolled down my cheeks. Jezebelle moved close and I leaned into her, resting my forehead on her nose. Long moments passed as I sobbed into her soft coat.

"He's never going to know, is he?" I asked her. "I'm going to leave and he'll never know how I feel."

Jezebelle whinnied quietly.

"I can't even tell him now, because of that girl," I said. "But I can say it to you, Jezebelle."

I stood up straight, my hand still on her nose. "Quinn Daniel Claremont, I am madly in love with you. I have been all my life. And I always will be!"

A sound in the stable made me jump away from my horse. God! Were they back? And laughing at me for my pronouncement? My face flamed. I couldn't bear it.

I turned, chin high, ready to stay strong and bold. At least now Quinn would know.

But the figure standing by the feed room door wasn't Quinn.

It was Bennett, his older brother.

"Sorry to startle you," he said smoothly.

My cheeks burned again. I barely knew Bennett, but Quinn had always told me how uptight he was. *Couldn't have a bit of fun if you paid him to do it.*

"I was just saying good-bye to my horse," I said.

Bennett nodded. "She's a lovely mare." He stepped toward the stall.

His nearness made my skin prickle. Bennett was formidable, tall and imposing. He didn't wear jeans, not ever, and loomed over me in his khakis and sport coat.

He smelled expensive, like aftershave and fresh linen. His eyes flitted over my outfit, and I had to resist the urge to cover myself.

His hand slid down Jezebelle's nose. For some reason, the sight of his long fingers trailing along her muzzle made me shiver. A tingling sensation ran through my body.

"We'll take good care of her for you," he said.

He knew I was leaving? I couldn't imagine he had time to pay any mind to the actions of the dance teacher's illegitimate daughter. I felt my station acutely. I had nothing, and he had everything. My own mother's livelihood depended on him now that his retched old father was gone. Bennett ran the family business and kept the estate.

"Thank you," I finally managed to say. "She's a good horse."

"I hear you have your mother's talent," he said. "I'm sure you will do well."

I took a few steps back. "Thank you again," I said. Maybe he hadn't heard anything I had said about Quinn. I was eager to get away.

I had only just begun to turn when he said, "My brother is not who you think he is."

The fire that had recently set my face aflame burst hot. "Of course he is. I've known him since I was born! I know everything about him!" It wasn't true, but it felt true. I hadn't missed a single one of his birthdays. I was there when he learned to ride. When he broke his arm falling off the back fence. When he buried his father.

I wanted to say these things, but Bennett's gaze dropped to my thin shirt again. I wanted to slap him. But I stood there as he took me in, my tiny shorts, muscled dancer's legs, and bare feet. I wasn't sure which I felt more like — a street beggar or a prostitute.

Bennett finally brought his eyes back to my face. "I'm sure if he'd felt tempted, he would have come to you," he said. "Be glad he considers you the kid play-mate. Your heart is still in one piece."

My head wanted to explode with things to say to defend Quinn. But this was my mother's boss. She loved it here. I couldn't ruin it for her.

So instead, I ran through the stable and back to my little room.

Tomorrow, the rest of my life would begin.

Chapter Three

Six Years Later

THE TAXI PULLED AWAY, ITS TIRES CRUNCHING AS IT circled the giant fountain in front of the main entrance to the estate.

I could have gone around to the back, where staff and deliveries came in. It was much closer to my mother's guesthouse. Technically I was here to see her.

But my visit home was also about Quinn. My life had changed a lot in the six years since I left. But my longing for him would not die. It affected everything. I hadn't managed to have a relationship that lasted more than a week. As soon as the man wasn't Quinn-like, my heart shriveled like the Grinch. My iPhone had more blocked numbers than a retired call girl.

So I was home. During my break between ballet seasons, I was going to get him out of my head, one way or another.

The hot breeze ruffled the tendrils escaping my intricate braided updo. I had forgotten how hot San Antonio could be in the summer. If I stood out here very long, sweat would wilt my sharp Versace suit. Already my feet felt pinched in the four-inch Louboutins.

This was stupid. What was I thinking? Showing up in fancy clothes and pricey shoes? I was just a kid playing dress-up.

The urgency to get away from the big double doors became intense. I did not want to be seen stalking the front like a crazed fan. I needed to do this the right way. Establish myself in the guesthouse. Practice ballet with my mother. Find out why she missed my last show. And watch Quinn from a distance until I figured out what to do about this annoying never-ending crush.

Time to trudge around to the back where I belonged.

I picked up the handle of one of the bags and tilted it down to roll. I shouldn't have worn the spike heels. Now I would suffer in them while I wheeled my luggage down the path in the heat.

But it had been a nice illusion, even for just a moment.

I paused. Might as well get the full effect before I gave it up. I closed my eyes and pictured another Juliet, one whose social standing would attract someone like Quinn, pulling up in an expensive chauffeured car. The butler would open the doors and greet me, sending out his young staff member to take my bags. I'd be escorted inside and given a cocktail on the patio. Quinn would come down, pleased to see me.

Stop.

I had to stop.

Enough.

I reached for the second suitcase. I had traveled as light as I could, but this was a monthlong stay. So I had a lot.

As I tried to maneuver the two bags, the strap of my purse slid off my shoulder. I let go of a suitcase, and it fell over onto the paved circle. The clever beaded charm that helped me identify my luggage smashed into pieces, the colored bits rolling across the ground.

Damn. Thankfully nobody was seeing the hot mess I was in front of the grand mansion.

I drew in a deep breath to steady myself. Nothing about this day was going to be easy. Coming back had turned me into a sniveling teen all over again.

And of course Mother didn't even know I was coming. But she hadn't explained why she missed my last performance in New York. Her evasion when I asked her left a tendril of unease in me. So I closed up the room in the walk-up I shared with three other girls and got on a plane.

I hadn't been back to San Antonio since I left. Mother always traveled to me, using her savings for grand trips to L.A. and Paris and Montreal to watch me dance. Holidays were busy with *The Nutcracker* or holiday fund-raising events.

I hadn't seen a need to come home. If this had ever been home.

But I worried Mother was out of money. Ballerinas at my level did not make a lot, especially living in the city, but I would try to help her if she'd let me.

I fastened my handbag to the handle of one of the suitcases. I'd come back to clean up the beads where they sat on the pristine gray drive like a Mardi Gras castoff. I had just gotten the luggage under control when the front doors of the estate flew open. A butler I had never seen before hurried out.

"I am so sorry, Miss Parker. We weren't expecting

you for another two hours. Did you take a taxi? We could have sent a car for you." He hurriedly motioned to a young man I didn't know to retrieve my bags.

"Oh!" I said. "I think there has been a mistake. I —"

I stopped short when Quinn appeared on the front porch in tennis gear. He rested a racket on his shoulder. "You're awfully dressed up for a tennis pro."

My voice didn't seem to work as I took him in. I was already flustered and not ready to see him yet. He was twenty-seven now, tan and muscled in the fitted shirt over loose shorts.

It was also a Tuesday afternoon. Didn't he work?

"Miss Parker, I'll escort you to your guesthouse," the butler said. "Would you like a golf cart to take you around?"

My lips were frozen. Quinn was staring right at me, but he didn't see me for who I was.

Should I try to pull this off? Tennis pro? He obviously didn't know this instructor very well. Maybe I resembled her picture.

I stood up straight, tugging on the bottom of the smart fitted jacket to my suit. We looked at each other, and I could see the interest in his eyes. He'd just broken off an engagement to some actress, I knew. I had a Google alert on his name.

He didn't look particularly devastated about it.

His gaze raked over my tawny gold jacket and matching skirt, down my legs to the achingly high Louboutins.

"Won't you come in for a quick drink before we hit the nets?" Quinn gestured to his outfit. "I had planned to lob a few balls before you arrived, but perhaps we could talk strategy first. Over some champagne? Or would that ruin our training regimen?"

I still couldn't speak. My heart hammered. He held out his hand to me. I itched to take it. It's what I'd always wanted.

The young man stood with my bags, waiting on my order. I could go in, see the ruse through. I wouldn't get far. The cook would spot me. Or one of the girls. Although if Quinn couldn't see it...

"Miss Parker?" the butler asked.

I was about to admit who I was when a glossy black Mercedes pulled up to the circle drive. Probably the real Miss Parker, and I was about to be outed.

I turned around, trying to decide if I should admit who I was or just let it happen.

But the driver was Bennett, Quinn's older brother.

"Oh, it's the boring brother," Quinn said. "Let's hurry before he spoils all the fun. I'll tell you straight out, he was not thrilled about my idea of bringing a tennis pro out full-time."

Quinn had always disparaged Bennett's seriousness, but back then it was always playful. Now his words had an edge to them.

My voice didn't want to work, and the explanation about who I was stuck in my throat. The moments hurtled by as Bennett stepped out of the car.

Quinn moved from the doorway to stand beside me. I turned to him, thinking surely now that he was close he would see who I was.

"I'm happy to walk you to your cottage myself," he said. When his hand touched my elbow, I positively glowed.

If only I could keep up this ruse a little longer!

Bennett headed up the steps. He nodded to the butler. "Hello, Adams," he said to him. He glanced at me. "Hello, Juliet. Nice to have you back."

Then he went inside.

My face blasted hot. He knew me! Now what would happen?

Quinn's head snapped around. "Juliet?"

I forced a smile. "In the flesh!"

God, had I really said that? Like I was twelve?

Quinn stared hard at my face. "This is unreal! It's like you're somebody else."

"Still me!" I said. I reached forward to take one of

my suitcases from the butler's assistant, who stood waiting for me to tell him what to do. "I'll handle this. I have to go around the wall."

The butler still looked quizzically at me. He had resumed a more formal position now that the crisis seemed to be over.

"I'm Danika's daughter," I told him.

His eyebrows raised as he realized the situation.

I couldn't stand any of this one moment more. Despite the smart suit, the high heels, the perfect hair, I was still the hired help's daughter. I snatched my luggage away and took off down the side path that led around the wall.

I heard Quinn say, "Wait!" but there wasn't enough conviction in it for me. He was the one who didn't respond to my emails in the first months I was gone.

I was the one who saw picture after picture of the women he'd been with during all these years.

I was so stupid. So stupid.

I ran faster, the wheels on the luggage bouncing as I dragged them down the path.

Only when I had turned the corner past the wall did I stop to take a breath. My feet were used to taking a beating, but the pounding of my heart had nothing to do with the run.

I peeked back around the wall.

Quinn and the butler were heading inside. Quinn tapped his racket on the ground as he walked, as if agitated.

I leaned against the stone. Despite six years of accomplished dance, my acceptance into a ballet troupe that traveled internationally, and my advancement from the chorus to minor roles, I had gotten nowhere.

I was still the girl peering at the party from behind the wall.

Chapter Four

The path to Mother's guesthouse had never felt longer. I had no chance to enjoy getting reacquainted with the paths and trees that were my playground as a child.

I wanted to hide.

Not that Quinn was going to come looking for me. He was obviously expecting some fresh female tennis instructor. A live-in, no less. Now that I thought about it, his hand on my elbow was more creepy than titillating. Did he hit on everyone that way? Had he always? He obviously didn't know the woman or he would have realized I wasn't her.

By the time I arrived at the front door, the estate cook was already heading my way, her short legs a blur beneath her ample body in a blue dress and white apron. "Juliet?" she called. "Is that you?"

I arranged my luggage on the porch and waited for her, delighted to see the tiny woman who had worked here since before any of the Claremont children were born. "Yes, Amelia. So good to see you!"

Amelia was small and round and smelled of flour and vanilla, like a walking pastry. She pressed her palms to my cheeks. "You look so different! All grown up! And beautiful!"

"Thank you," I said. "Is Mother at the dance studio?"

"No, I believe she is out." A concerned emotion flitted across Amelia's face.

"I'm sure her schedule has changed. Rose is gone, right? To college? Only Pearl would still be here."

Amelia's smile was more forced now. "Miss Rose is in Europe traveling. Miss Pearl has little interest in dance these days."

"Oh." I worried that Mother's job was in jeopardy. Maybe that's why she didn't make it to New York. Saving her money.

I would have to adjust my plans. Base out of someplace less expensive than Manhattan. Find a studio that needed an instructor. Maybe we could buy her into one so she wasn't just working hourly as an instructor, but getting a percentage of the profits.

My mind raced.

"Don't you worry about anything," Amelia said.

She reached behind me to open Mother's door with her enormous set of keys. "You settle yourself right in. Will you be here long?"

"About a month," I said as I rolled the bags inside. "How did you know I was here?"

"Master Quinn," she said with a grin. "He was carrying on about you."

My heart sped up again. "What did he say?"

"Just that he'd seen you and that he couldn't believe it was you!"

I bit my lip. "How has he been? I heard he was engaged."

Amelia shook her head. "That boy. Engaged three times while you were gone! Three! Always asking. Then discarding. It's all the talk." She stuck her keys in her pocket. "You hungry? I can send a boy with something to eat."

"Not now, thank you," I said. The fact that she offered to send someone with food rather than have me come to the kitchen was not lost on me. Nothing had really changed at all. I was still meant to stay behind the wall.

"All right, honey. I will see you again real soon." She pinched my cheek as though I were still five. "Don't you worry your pretty head about anything."

I went inside the darkened living room. It was like a cave. Interesting. Mother always liked things filled with light. I raised the blinds and pushed aside the curtains.

Most everything was the same as six years ago. The wicker furniture with padded cushions. The colorful pillows and bright tapestries on the walls. I felt a surge of happiness. Mom had surrounded me with cheer. She had tried. I had been such a mess. Mooning over Quinn. Rarely leaving the estate other than for school.

I headed back to my old bedroom with the window that faced the stone wall. Everything was as I had left it. The white ruffled bedspread. The desk with a mirror. My closet had some new boxes in it, but the clothes I'd left behind were still there.

I sat on the bed. As much as I wanted to think of Quinn as creepy or intolerable, I couldn't. I remembered young Quinn, riding a horse beside me. Taking walks on the back lot of the estate. Brushing down Jezebelle.

Jezebelle!

I hurried for my bag to change out of the fancy clothes. I would go see my mare. A quick ride would certainly cheer me up.

The jeans I chose were soft and worn but well made. The summer heat meant a fitted tank top. I went with cherry red. I dug around in my closet and found my boots. Dried mud clung to the bottom and

I brushed my fingers against it. The mud was six years old. Part of my life before.

I hauled the boots out to the porch and banged them on the ground. The dirt broke away and scattered.

I felt a lot better, like I'd shaken away some doubts. When the boots were on, I took off in a sprint for the barn. Running through the grass took me back, way before my angsty teen crush and into my childhood. I remembered when I first saw Jezebelle on a bright clear spring afternoon. When Quinn had kissed me and the whole world had split wide.

This was home after all.

The double doors at the end of the stable were propped open. Off in the round pen, a trainer I didn't recognize was walking a yearling on a line. I should have asked Amelia who was still here that I would know. Mother sometimes mentioned the staff changes, but she always seemed leery of bringing up the estate, as if she didn't want me asking about Quinn.

Most of the doors were open, as the horses were out in the field. I double-checked Jezebelle's stall. Her bridle and bit hung in the back and the placard over the stall still bore her name.

My boots rang on the cement floor as I walked to

the other end to head out into the pens to locate her. I'd bring her back to saddle her.

The door to the break room opened and Sawyer, the barn manager, came out, pushing his hat down on his head. His darkly tanned skin was a little more grizzled, and the hair at his temples included a lot more gray.

He glanced up at me, then paused, as if trying to decide if he knew me.

I helped him out. "Sawyer, it's me! Juliet!"

With that, he broke out in a wide smile. "Jules! You're not a tyke anymore!"

I stepped into his wiry embrace. He'd always been tall and lean. And a bachelor to the core, although a rumor had gone around when I was a teen that he was sweet on the florist who came every Tuesday. He managed the barn and often broke the new horses himself.

"Where's my mare?" I asked.

"We just turned them all out," he said. "You want me to have someone fetch her for you?"

Funny how Sawyer was treating me like a guest when the others hadn't. "That's okay," I said. "I'll go track her down."

"Bennett's been riding her for you," he said. "She's in fine shape."

I headed out the back exit and climbed the gate

rather than opening it. It felt good to be outside. My lungs expanded and I took in a great gulp of air. I could breathe again. In New York I spent almost all my time indoors at rehearsals.

The horses were gathered around a water trough. I could see Jezebelle nosing her way alongside the others. She was gray-blue in the bright light and hadn't changed a bit.

I took a rope halter from a hook by the gate to bring her in. This was something I couldn't do in the city. While I loved the bright lights and lifestyle, I had definitely missed the slower pace of Texas. You couldn't just step outside to ride a horse in Chelsea.

I talked softly as I approached the trough. A black foal startled and spirited away with high anxious steps. The others looked at me with languid eyes.

"Jezebelle," I said. "Come."

Her ears twitched, as if she, too, wasn't sure what to make of this oddly familiar stranger. Then she lifted her nose and whinnied. I ran my hand along her mane. "It's just me, girl. Just Jules."

She seemed mollified as I slid the halter on and led her back to the stable and through the gate. Sawyer waited inside with her gear. "How long are you here for?" he asked as we saddled her up.

"A month," I said.

"I hear you're doing pretty well up there in New York. A ballerina and all."

I cinched the rigging and adjusted the stirrups. "It's been fun. Mother has come up for several shows."

"She sure is proud of you," Sawyer said. He patted Jezebelle on the rump. "Glad to see you up on your horse. We wondered if you were going to be all citified."

I laughed. "You can take the girl out of the country...," I said.

"Glad to see they haven't taken the country out of the girl."

My boot fit nicely in the stirrup, and I swung my leg over Jezebelle's back. "You ready, my lady?" I asked, rubbing her head.

She stepped lively as Sawyer walked ahead and opened the gate for us. "Take her out for a spell. Bennett likes to walk her on the trail."

I nodded, urging Jezebelle forward.

He'd mentioned Bennett twice now. There were a lot of horses in the barn. Bennett had a powerful former racehorse that was technically his. Or at least he used to. I wondered why he rode mine.

As we trotted out across the open pen, I thought about that last night when Bennett caught me confessing my love for Quinn to my horse. He *had* promised me she would be taken care of.

I just hadn't expected he would do it himself.

One of the horse handlers waved at me and jogged ahead to open the gate to the back lot. The trail through the mesquite trees and brush had been there since the estate had been a real ranch.

Prettying up the barn and cleaning up the grounds had transformed a working ranch into an estate. Maybe I'd hoped my clothes and poise would do the same for me.

But nobody was fooled. Least of all me.

Chapter Five

One thing about nature is that if nobody touches it, it doesn't change.

As Jezebelle picked her way along the trail, my heart soared with the recognition of each detail I'd treasured when I was a girl.

"There's the ghost tree," I told my horse, pointing toward a great towering oak with a giant knot in the bark that looked like a screaming woman.

"And elephant rock!" The big gray stone had a deep smooth indentation along a curve, leaving the impression of an elephant trunk.

Jezebelle tossed her head as if feeling my energy. I nudged her into a trot and the breeze cooled my face as we moved faster along the trail.

I wanted to shout out loud. My soul felt very full. The emotion was rare for me. Sometimes I felt it when I nailed the perfect pirouette or during a ballet, when I became completely, almost supernaturally, in sync with a line of dancers.

But this was so much easier.

The very idea made me laugh. It was true. I had to work very hard for the happy moments in New York. The rehearsal and performance schedule was grueling. The relationships between the dancers vacillated wildly between best friends to cutthroat competition. The travel was exhausting and yet you had to perform no matter how you felt, jet-lagged or not sure about the foreign food or down with a cold.

This happiness was effortless. Jezebelle was doing all the work.

I ducked beneath a sprig of a tree branch that jutted out into the trail. When I lifted my head, Jezebelle suddenly slowed.

"What is it, girl?"

We rounded a curve and I saw him.

Face to face.

Horse to horse.

Bennett.

Serious as always.

I drew Jezebelle up short. Bennett also halted his racehorse.

We ended up side by side, facing opposite directions. Like the night I left, Bennett's gaze slid down my body, taking in the red tank top and jeans.

"You left behind the suit," he said.

"So did you."

He glanced down at his riding outfit. No cowboy look here. All water-wicking advanced outdoor wear. It fit him like a second skin.

He was muscled and way more buff than I would have pegged a businessman like him to be. He must take his workouts as seriously as he did the company.

"Not very Texas of you," I said.

He shrugged. "I don't wear togas in Rome either."

I had nothing to say to that. Jezebelle nickered and pranced, feeling anxious so close to the stallion. I drew up the reins and patted her neck.

Bennett shifted his horse over a little. "It looks like New York agreed with you." His eyes slid over me again.

My body zinged with a tremor that moved from stirrups to reins. I tried not to stare at his thighs bulging on either side of the horse. "Thank you."

"You here for long?" he asked.

"About a month."

His eyebrows lifted, and I remembered that same surprised expression from the last night before I left town. My face burned remembering my pronouncement about my love for Quinn. And Bennett's response that his brother wasn't who I thought he was.

"That's a nice visit," he said. "Did you take a leave from your troupe?"

"We have a break between seasons," I said.

Bennett sat back on his saddle. He seemed pleased that I was staying. My brain couldn't comprehend why. He had been only marginally tolerant of my friendship with Quinn when we were kids.

The racehorse danced a few steps, annoyed with the stillness. But Bennett persisted. "You sure surprised everyone, showing up like you did."

Now it felt like he was stalling. He wanted to keep talking to me? We had about as much in common as a duke and a parlor maid.

"I'm hoping no one will tip off my mom." I tilted my head. "Can I count on your discretion?"

A slow smile spread across his face. "Scout's honor."

I laughed. "You were never a Boy Scout. I was here, you know!"

His grin revealed a dimple I'd never seen on his cheek. "You were." Then his expression sobered. His voice was completely serious as he said, "You were here all along."

The change in tone was unsettling. Jezebelle felt my discomfort and lifted her nose, fighting the tightly held reins. I stroked her long neck. "Well, thank you for keeping the secret," I said. "I'm going to keep my ride short to make sure I don't miss her."

Our eyes clashed again and the moment lengthened. I was about to break the intensity when we heard the unmistakable thunder of a running horse coming up the trail.

"What the hell?" Bennett said with a curse. He nudged his horse forward and motioned me to follow him into the brush. We were on a curve and whoever was hightailing it along the narrow trail would run us right over if we didn't get out of the way.

The horses shifted with unease as the sound grew louder. Bennett had to duck to avoid getting entangled with a low branch overhead. "If it's one of the trainers, I'll have their head on a platter," he said.

Sitting under the tree on horses, waiting on the arrival of some mad rider, made me feel like we were in a knights-of-the-round-table movie. "This is crazy," I whispered to Bennett.

He laughed quietly. "I feel like Robin Hood."

I watched him hunkered down over his horse. This was sort of fun. With Bennett. Who would have guessed that?

The ground thudded as the rider got closer. I half expected to see a man in black armor by the time the bushes began to quiver.

But when the horse came around the curve, it was someone we both knew quite well.

Quinn.

He was going so fast that when he saw us, he couldn't stop immediately. He drew up on the reins with a "Whooooa!" but was well past us by the time he got his horse to stop.

"I should have guessed," Bennett said under his breath. He eased forward, ducking under the branch.

What was Quinn doing out here?

I followed Bennett back out onto the trail. It wasn't wide enough for two to ride, so I halted behind him.

Quinn circled back around. His expression showed his displeasure at seeing his brother. "What are you doing out here?" he asked. "Don't you have some memos to dictate?"

"I always take a trail ride on Tuesdays," Bennett said evenly.

"With Juliet?"

"Now, that doesn't seem possible since she only just arrived an hour ago." Bennett's voice remained calm and smooth.

Jezebelle seemed unnerved by the tension between the brothers. I had to pay attention to keep her calm, patting her and pulling the reins. "The trail

49

seems a little crowded," I said. "I'm going to head back."

Both brothers said, "WAIT!" at the same time.

I took a few steps back with Jezebelle. "Are you two okay?"

Quinn forced his horse forward, nudging Bennett's aside. His stallion snorted with annoyance.

"Juliet," Quinn said. "I came out here to find you. Sawyer said you'd headed out on the trail."

My heart sped up. "You came tearing out here like a bat out of hell to find me?"

Bennett's horse snorted again as if he didn't buy it either. Quinn nudged his horse closer to me. "Yes. I couldn't leave it like it was. I wanted to talk to you. We used to ride together all the time."

The sound coming from Bennett's direction wasn't his horse this time. "I'll be on my way," he said. His eyes met mine. "Be careful out here." He looked right at his brother. "Mesquite trees have thorns."

He pushed past Quinn and eased around Jezebelle to head back toward the stable. When he was clear of us, he pushed the racehorse into a run.

"Glad we got that unpleasantness behind us," Quinn said. "I had no idea he still rode."

I glanced down at his tennis gear. His bare knees were already red from rubbing against the horse.

"You must have decided to saddle up at the last minute."

He frowned down at his legs. "Probably not my smartest move. But I couldn't wait."

My throat felt thick. Quinn was that desperate to get to me?

"Don't you have your tennis pro coming?" I asked.

"Adams can get her settled," Quinn said. "I hated how we left things."

I wasn't sure what he meant. From the driveway? Or our friendship? Or that last night I was here, when he took off with the blond girl?

I didn't have the courage to ask.

"Let's ride," Quinn said. "Slowly, so I can go easy on my knees."

"You're crazy," I said, but I backed up so he could turn around on the trail.

"It's worth it," he said with a lazy grin.

He led us through the brush and out into the wide open field that had once been used for growing hay. Now it was wild and weedy with tall thin grass, burnt on the ends from the blistering summer sun.

"I remember the days we used to come out here," Quinn said. "Things were so damn easy then."

I turned my face to the sunshine. Despite the tension of a few minutes ago, everything about this moment was perfect. The smell of dirt and grass.

Birds caw-cawing and the beat of their wings. The soft whinnies of the horses.

"Now that's a picture," Quinn said. He watched me from the middle of the field.

"What is?"

"You. A glorious bit of wild color in a sea of grass," he said. "Soaking up all this beauty."

His eyes on me made everything hum. I was acutely aware of the saddle beneath me, my knees locked against the horse.

I nudged Jezebelle forward. The two horses walked amicably together, side by side. A rabbit ran out ahead, pausing every few feet as if checking to see if we followed. With each step, a cluster of grasshoppers leaped out of our way.

I had forgotten this.

It was all so mixed up. My childhood. Nature. Getting away. And Quinn. Was he here as my friend again?

He wasn't looking at me as a friend. His eyes were hot, his glance falling on key parts of my body.

I could barely stand the tension. "Remember that time we decided to have a campout here in this field?" I asked. "We thought we'd be able to sneak the horses out."

Quinn laughed, and the moment eased. "There was more security on that barn than Fort Knox," he said. "When we tried going through the break room window, we set off the alarm and the cops came out."

"Your dad was so mad," I said.

"We didn't get to ride."

I adjusted my reins. "We did manage to have our night under the stars a little later, though," I said.

"Did we?" Quinn looked at me quizzically.

My joy dropped a notch as I realized he didn't remember. It had been an emotional night for me. I was fourteen and just starting to figure out what all these feelings I had meant. Quinn had just come back from a party, seventeen and starting to rebel against his strict father.

I knew he was outside. I often lay on the top of the wall, watching the various Claremonts drive in and out of the six-car garage. Quinn had a little black Porsche. Mom had gone to bed hours before, and I waited for Quinn to come home. He'd already started to pull away, running off with his older friends. He only made time for me when he was stuck at home for one punishment or another. But that time mattered.

He was late getting in, and he and his father had a big argument. When the garage closed, his father made a big show of changing the code on the bay with the Porsche so Quinn couldn't get his car back out.

I waited. I knew Quinn, and when he was upset, he couldn't stay inside the walls. So when he angrily evaded the house and went out onto the patio, I raced to the stables.

When he came out the back gate, I was sitting on a stack of hay bales.

"What are you doing up so late?" he asked.

"Couldn't sleep," I said.

"Well, come on," he said. "I could use some company."

The horses were as inaccessible as they always were back when his dad was alive, so we'd walked the trail that night, guided only by the light of the moon. When we got to this field, we dropped into the grass. Quinn stared into the sky, and I had watched him. I could barely contain the intensity of emotion I felt for him.

We didn't talk or anything, just lay out there under the stars in silence. He fell asleep finally, and I dared, that one time only, to inch close to him until my head touched his shoulder. He'd shifted and pulled me in.

But he didn't remember that now.

And I couldn't forget.

I got off Jezebelle and walked, holding her reins. Quinn dismounted and followed my lead. After a while he said, "Hey, let's walk with just us."

We tied the horses to a tree and took off back across the field. The grass was up to my knees and I held out my hand to allow the tips to tickle my palm.

"How was New York?" he asked.

I wanted to lash out, tell him he didn't know because he never answered my emails. Those first few months were hell, and lonely, and painful and hard. I had no one. The dancers were hard to get to know. And the few girls I was friends with back home had moved on to college or settled into jobs. A friend dancing in New York wasn't someone they could talk to.

But I couldn't say all that. I settled on something easy.

"Being a dancer is hard work," I said. "But the city is exciting. A big change from here."

I closed my hand around one of the blades of grass and tore it away. I held it to my nose, smelling the sharp scent of it, like a mown lawn. There were no lawns in Manhattan, not the places I went.

Quinn also plucked some grass and sniffed. "Is this supposed to do something?" he asked.

"I don't smell grass a lot," I said. "If you want to sit on some, you have to go to Central Park. Most of the other parks are all concrete."

"Sounds dismal," he said. "Although the times I've been there, parks weren't high on the agenda."

"So you've been?" I asked. I squashed the disappointment that he hadn't let me know. "I could have gotten you tickets."

I could picture him in the clubs and pricey restaurants. Staying in suites at the tippy top of hotels in Times Square.

"Just once or twice," he said. He stopped and reached for my arm. "If I had known, I would have flown up every weekend."

I flushed with anger. "Known what? That I wasn't a kid anymore?"

Quinn drew me against him. He wrapped his arms around me and pressed my head against his shoulder.

I wanted to be angry, but the feel of him against me was so right. I'd longed for it since I was a girl.

And now the moment had come.

I wondered wildly if he would kiss me. If we'd keep going and undress in the field. I pictured Quinn's body over mine in the grass and the need for him bolted through me so hard that I shuddered in his arms.

"I know," he said. "I was terrible. I was a rotten friend."

Friend.

Of course.

Friends. We were friends.

I pulled away. "It's all right," I said. I couldn't look

at him, but headed toward my horse. "I'm sure you were busy."

My boots crushed the grass.

Quinn hurried to catch up. "You okay, Jules?"

"Fine," I said, scrambling for a safe topic until I could get to Jezebelle and go. "Are you working at your father's company?"

"It's mine and Bennett's company now. Mostly Bennett's. He bought out all our sisters' shares. I've kept mine, mainly just to piss him off."

I couldn't look at him, just kept trudging toward the trees. "So you're working there?"

"Something like that. Juliet. Wait." His voice was plaintive.

I stopped. But I couldn't turn around. I was still struggling to contain all the things I was feeling. Need. Disappointment. Anticipation. Hope.

His hand touched my shoulder.

Maybe now it would happen. He'd turn me around. We'd kiss. He'd see that I'd always loved him. He'd know.

But if he didn't feel it too, what then? How would I go on another month here?

"Will you look at me?" he asked.

The days piled up ahead of me. I was here to see my mother. Quinn would do his tennis lessons. I remembered his hand on my arm when he thought I was her. He had plans. Whatever was going on between us wasn't part of that plan.

I would not turn around.

"I have to see if my mother is home," I said and untied Jezebelle from the tree. My boot slipped as I missed the stirrup. I tried again and this time got my leg over the horse.

Quinn stepped aside. "Hey."

I didn't trust myself to look at him. I tugged on Jezebelle's reins and said, "I'm sure I'll see you around."

"Juliet," he said. "I'm sorry I didn't write you. It was crappy of me."

"It's okay," I said. "I survived." And with that, I pushed Jezebelle into a light run. I couldn't get away fast enough.

Bennett was right. I had already been pricked by the thorns.

Chapter Six

Sawyer took Jezebelle to her stall for a cool down and I raced back to Mother's house. Quinn didn't chase me down. I didn't even see him on the trail. Probably he was having to walk his horse due to his silly choice to wear shorts to ride.

It seemed romantic at the moment, but now I wondered if the man had a lick of common sense.

The house was quiet and still. I pulled off my boots and wondered if I would have time for a shower before Mom showed. I jerked the pins out of my braids and began unraveling them. My hair was impossibly long and all one length to keep it easy to tie up for shows.

I rarely ever let it down. The cascading waves of black fell past my shoulders, kinked from the braids. I ran my fingers through it.

The pictures in the hallway were arranged the same as always. Me as a baby. Me and Mom. Riding Jezebelle. My graduation.

Except.

A picture of me and Quinn by the barn had been replaced by one of me onstage. I frowned and took the frame off the wall.

The back opened with a flick of the latch. Sure enough, beneath the image of my role in *The Nutcracker* was the old one.

I was about nine. Quinn would have been twelve. He was lanky and awkward, but still handsome in that cute way confident boys could be. We were sitting on the ever-present bales of hay outside the barn. Quinn held a pitchfork as if he was actually going to spread out the hay. Maybe he did. In his younger days, he liked working out at the barn. He was always looking for an excuse to escape the difficult atmosphere of the estate.

Next to him, I sat skinny and happy in jeans and a plaid shirt that tied at the waist. My ponytail was off to one side, making me look sassy.

I pulled the picture out of the frame before hanging the new one back on the wall. It could come with me if Mother wasn't able to handle looking at it.

I'd just tucked it in one of my bags when I heard the front door open. Time for the surprise.

My footsteps were silent as I headed up the hall. Mom moved toward the kitchen with a grocery sack. Then she saw my purse on the coffee table and paused.

She looked up, quizzically, and saw me standing at the entrance to the room. She almost dropped the bag, but caught it and set it on the floor.

"Juliet!" Her hand came to her mouth.

As I moved closer, my concern began to grow. She wasn't well. Her head was wrapped in a scarf even though it was ninety degrees out. And she was thin. More than thin.

"Mom?" I took her hand. She wore a fluttery shirt that came down below her elbows. When she moved, I saw the bruises on the inside of her arm. I touched her wrist. "What is this?"

She pulled away. "Just some treatments I was getting. It's all done now."

I touched her head. "You have cancer?"

Her watery eyes met mine. "I was going to tell you."

My panic rose into a flood of emotion. "When?"

"I couldn't affect your dance season. I wanted to see how chemo would go."

"How is it?" I wasn't sure why my voice was even working, except through sheer adrenaline. The drumbeat of fear banged in my skull.

"It went just fine," she said. "I mean, as fine as something like that goes. I'm just waiting on the tests to see how well it worked."

"Where? How? When?" I couldn't move. My whole world had narrowed.

"Let's sit down," she said. "Let me put the milk away."

She picked up the bag again and took it to the kitchen. Her movements were pained and slow. My heart hit the floor. She was sick, and she hadn't even told me.

I sank onto a cushion on the sofa, trying to breathe. My chest felt so tight.

Mom returned with a glass of water. "Drink this. One thing I've learned when the going gets tough is to stay hydrated."

I accepted the cool glass and took a sip. It did help calm me.

She sat beside me. "I was diagnosed about three months ago."

"Three months!"

She held up a hand. "I know. But you had just started rehearsals for *La Bayadère*. No one should ever miss the opportunity to perform the Kingdom of the Shades. And you would have."

I took another drink of water. She was right. I would have come down. And lost my spot.

"I'm doing fine," she said, patting my leg. "I wouldn't have you miss your big moments over my little malady."

"How bad is it?" I asked.

"Just a simple lymphoma," she said. "Perfectly treatable."

I didn't know much of anything about cancer beyond the pink ribbons. "So you will be all right?"

She managed a smile. "I will be perfectly all right. So tell me why you are here."

"It's the season break," I said. "And you didn't come to see *La Bayadère*. You missed the Shades."

She nodded. "I know. I wasn't well enough to fly to New York."

"And you still wouldn't tell me."

"It seemed like you wouldn't need to know." She straightened the fluttery sleeve. "I thought I would be fine by the time I saw you and could show off my chic short haircut." She touched the scarf. "It's coming back."

I leaned back against the cushion. "Does the staff know? Amelia? Sawyer?"

"Yes," she said. "And Bennett, since I wasn't always able to work with Pearl."

I sat up. "Did Quinn?"

Her lips tightened. "I don't know. We don't exactly cross paths. Bennett comes to see me and asks about Pearl's lessons. And he oversees the health plan for the staff. So he knew."

"Is it expensive? Can you manage?" I thought wildly about the meager contents of my bank accounts. But I could get a loan. Reduce expenses.

"Juliet, it's fine. I'm fine. The estate has taken care of me."

Thank God. I wanted to go track down Bennett and throw my arms around him. But the way he had acted on the trail...maybe not.

This was all so confusing.

She reached for a long lock of my hair. "So lovely. You so rarely have it down. I didn't think much of mine until it was gone."

I tried to imagine the glossy black strands falling out in her hands. I felt queasy and set the water on the coffee table.

"How long do you plan to stay?" she asked.

"I have a month of leave."

"That's quite a while!" She tucked her arm around mine, sitting close on the sofa. "What should we do?"

"Are you still dancing?" I asked. I was afraid of the answer. Who was my mother without her dance?

"I am," she said. "Should we head to the studio?"

I nodded, holding back tears. Dancing together would help. I would see she wasn't lost. And maybe I could let go of some of my fear.

Chapter Seven

Mom and I moved with slow synchronicity in the studio. The floor had been resurfaced, glossy and smooth with new wood planks.

I knew this space well. The placement of the barre, the lines between the panes of mirrors on the wall. Light poured in from overhead windows that ran the full length of the building on two sides.

I felt at home here.

The song ended and Mother dropped her ankle from the barre. "I don't get out here as much as I once did," she said.

"Is Pearl dancing at all?" I asked.

"No, not really." She wrapped a towel around her neck and walked over to the stereo system to shut off the music.

"But they keep you employed here?"

"Bennett still takes lessons," she said.

"Bennett?" I tried to picture him in tights and almost fell off the barre.

"He likes ballroom dancing," she said. She sank onto a chair in the corner.

I looked away. She was painfully thin in her leotard. We had only done barre work, stretches and arm positions. I sensed she wasn't up for much more.

"I remember him doing Cotillion," I said. "He thought it was torture."

"Young boys don't like being forced to learn to dance," she said. "But men realize it is the easiest way to draw a woman close."

"So he's keeping you on here just to teach ballroom?" My concern hadn't abated. I couldn't have my mother be both sick and unemployed. I moved to the floor to continue stretching.

"I also do yoga for the staff. And two of the former Mrs. Claremonts stayed on-site for a few months a year or so ago. They wanted to do dance workouts." She got up to press on my back to deepen the stretch.

"Really?" The Claremont patriarch had been married six times. The first woman had been a dancer, I knew. She had died during an emergency C-section, along with the child.

After that, Claremont had seemed to want to

ensure such a tragedy never hit him a second time. He would find a socially climbing woman, marry her with an iron-clad pre-nup, have a child, and then divorce her. Each one had to choose between the child and the money, and each one had chosen the money.

By the time he died, just a few years before I left, he had five motherless children.

"Which Mrs. Claremonts were they?" I asked. "And wasn't there a rule against them visiting?"

"Numbers five and six," Mom said. She began moving me through our old floor-stretch routine, her fingers touching my arm or back lightly to remind me which position to take. "Bennett relaxed the rule because Rose and Pearl were doing so badly. Cutting school and not coming home."

"Did it help?" I exhaled into position, my nose at my knees.

"Hardly. These women are only twenty years older than the girls. They took them clubbing. Bennett sent them packing again."

Mom tapped my shoulder, signaling it was time to move to the next part of the workout. I smiled at how we fell into it so easily, as if the six years had never passed.

"ONE two three FOUR five six," she counted as I ran across the floor, executing a grand jeté.

"Glorious," Mom said, her voice cracking.

I paused. "You okay?"

"You're so good," she said. "Seeing you here, where you used to dance, it's so obvious." She pressed her hands against her cheeks. "I may have held you back. I should have sent you to school so much sooner."

I hurried across the gleaming floor and pressed my hands against hers. "Of course not. I did just fine."

"But you could be a principal by now," she said.

"Maybe," I said. "Those roles aren't just about the quality of the dance. It's political."

She nodded. "I never knew. I never got that far."

I let go of her. "You're not letting me off the workout hook that easy, are you?" I asked.

Mom shook her head. "Back to position," she smiled. "Three more."

I focused back in, intent on pleasing her. Each muscle, each position of my body, each preparatory hold before I unleashed became an acute point of attention.

I went into a series of arabesques, part of the Shades dance that I knew she would recognize, then the door opened with a bang.

"Dump them in here," a voice said.

I turned to face the source of the noise.

It was Pearl, sixteen and heavily made up. She wore a pair of ripped jeans and three tank tops of varying colors, the top one loose and strategically cut up.

A delivery man in a brown uniform unloaded a stack of boxes from a dolly.

"Don't block the door, thank you," Mother said.

The man shifted the boxes over.

"Nobody uses this place anyway," Pearl said.

My anger rose up like a furnace blast. "What exactly are we doing right now?" I asked.

"Who are you?" Pearl put her hand on her hip. Her long blond hair fell down one shoulder. It had black tips now.

"Juliet," I said. "And we're working out in here."

Her eyebrows went up in shock, taking in my dance outfit and hair.

The delivery man looked unsure now and slid the base of the dolly back under a box.

Pearl kicked it off again. "They are just the help," she said. "I've got a lot more stuff coming and no place to put it."

"You have an entire mansion," I said, but Mom placed her hand on my shoulder.

"It's fine, Pearl," she said. "When is your party?"

"It's not my party, it's Quinn's," Pearl said. "For

that tennis chick. I just got stuck dealing with the decorations."

My stomach dropped a little to hear that there was a party. Quinn hadn't mentioned it on our ride. I remembered again his hand on my arm when he thought I was the tennis instructor.

"I was just wondering how long the boxes would be here," Mom said. She moved away from me to shift them against the wall. The delivery man took one glance at her frailty and moved forward to help.

"The party's Friday," Pearl said.

"It will be fine," Mom said. "Will you be at your lesson later today?"

"Hardly," Pearl said. "I've got way better things to do."

She sneered at me, as if to say, "And you don't."

I had nothing to prove to her. I turned away to refocus.

Step step step, LEAP. Step step step, LEAP. By the time I was winded, Pearl and her delivery man were gone.

Mom held out a towel and I took it. "Lovely girl," I said.

"It's hard growing up without a mother," she said. "Clarence Claremont really did his children a great disservice."

"They had a good nanny," I said, remembering the

warm, rotund, friendly faced Mrs. B. She had stayed on with the family until Pearl went to kindergarten.

"Which is probably the only reason they aren't psychopaths," Mom said.

This made me laugh. I had never heard her say anything like that.

I draped my arm around her. "Come on," I told her. "I'm dying for a cheese enchilada from Rose's Tamale House. You can't get decent Mexican food in Manhattan, at least not without paying fifty dollars for it."

"Fifty dollars! An enchilada plate is five!"

"Yep," I said. "And I'm buying."

We scooted between the boxes of decorations and headed out into the sweltering San Antonio summer afternoon. But I was on alert now. Mom had it tough enough. I wasn't going to let some billionaire's snotty daughter make her life any harder than it already was.

Chapter Eight

Even if Pearl hadn't announced the upcoming party, I would have known about it the next day. The bustle on the estate increased tenfold. The landscapers unloaded equipment to spruce up the grounds. And new patio furniture arrived and cushions were replaced.

The exterior windows were cleaned and the circle drive power-washed.

These were always the services that came out in the days leading up to one of the big events.

Mother spent a lot of the day sleeping, so I wandered the grounds in distinctly non–New York clothing, digging cutoff shorts and tank tops from the dregs of my closet. They fit differently now. I was leaner and more muscled, yet my hips were wider. I looked like something from a Jessica

Simpson music video. But why not? Nobody saw me anyway.

I took long walks. Despite my vow not to sit on the wall, I sometimes did, lying on my back, watching the workers make an already-perfect-looking lawn even more perfect. I laughed out loud when I spotted a man spraying a brown spot in the corner with green paint. How ridiculous!

I told myself I wasn't watching for Quinn, justifying my watchdog position because I wanted to find Bennett. I needed to thank him for looking after Mother. She would be in a real lurch if he hadn't been kind enough to keep her on. Even taking ballroom lessons himself.

I admitted my heart warmed at the thought of it, and wondered if he was any good at dance.

But Bennett was seriously scarce. I hadn't seen him come in last night, and he must have left so early this morning that he beat my sunrise run.

I shifted to lie on my side on the wall. Being up here felt comfortable and familiar. Maybe I was wrong to think I should even try to belong inside the estate. Very few people lived a lifestyle like the Claremonts and most were perfectly happy without it.

And truthfully, I wasn't sure how happy the people *inside* the wall were. Pearl definitely looked miserable.

Quinn came out to the back patio, and I sat up straight, then realized he might see me and collapsed back down on the wall.

He wore tennis gear and held a racket zipped up in a case. The courts were inside the wall, off in the far left corner from the French doors, beyond the pools and gardens. He headed that direction. He had a little bounce in his step, as though everything was going his way. Despite everything, my heart squeezed.

About that time, the back gate opened and a young woman with a black ponytail hurried across the lawn. She also carried a racket and wore a sunny yellow tennis skirt and tight white shirt.

This must be the tennis pro.

I watched her smooth her skirt and adjust her visor before calling out to Quinn. She seemed to have more on her mind than practice. And why wouldn't she? It wasn't every day you got called to live on an estate and train a hunky charming billionaire.

He turned around and smiled at her, hand uplifted in greeting. My stomach dipped as it always had when I watched Quinn with the dozens of women he'd entertained inside the walls. It was seriously silly that I had even imagined that he'd seemed interested during the ride yesterday.

Although he *had* ridden out to find me. In shorts.

Still, the proof was there. Quinn waited while the

girl caught up with him. Then he draped his arm around her shoulders.

That didn't look too professional.

Plus, he was throwing a *party* for her. And no small one, by the looks of it.

She gazed up at him with the usual *oh-how-I-adore-you* look, and I had to stop torturing myself. I lay on my back, eyes on the branches overhead. Eventually I started hearing the distant pong-plink of the ball on the court.

God, I was so stupid.

And now I couldn't leave. Not with Mom so sick. I would just have to tough out the month. Maybe we could find something else for Mom to do. Choreography. Or studio management. Something that wouldn't tax her.

Except it was easy for her here. And she had people looking after her.

Damn.

A car door slammed. I couldn't see the front drive from back here, so I stood up and walked along the top of the wall to the corner, holding on to tree branches as I went.

Bennett had pulled up to the circle and was heading for the front door. I could catch him if I hurried.

I couldn't wait to call out or I'd miss him, so I

shouted, "Bennett!" right as I leaped from the wall, over the hedge, and onto the walkway.

His step faltered as he saw me fly through the air.

"Wow," he said when I was close enough to hear. "You're like a bird."

I laughed. "When you have the equivalent of a drill sergeant shouting at you to defy gravity in a tutu, you get good at it."

He paused by the door, a leather briefcase slung over his shoulder by a long strap. Behind him, one of the staff members drove Bennett's car to the detached garage.

"I wanted to talk to you," I said. "About Mom."

He turned to me then. "Is she all right?"

My gaze dropped to his perfectly shined Italian leather shoes. I saw a lot of shoes like that at fundraisers for the ballet. "She said you know about her cancer."

"Yes. Her treatments seem to be going well." He took a step closer, which had the intended effect. I looked up at him.

His face was etched with concern. A breeze ruffled the brown hair that was a couple shades darker than his brother's. He wasn't hunky gorgeous like Quinn. But handsome in a distinguished way.

"Do you intend to keep her here, even though Pearl refuses lessons?"

He exhaled in a rush, as if thinking about his youngest sister was a great trial. "Pearl could use some grace and beauty, but she's off the rails. I don't even know how to pull her back."

"She'll be eighteen before too long anyway."

"And come into a lot of money," Bennett said. "That's never good."

"I wouldn't know," I said. I scrambled to pay for my crowded apartment. Thankfully we were given outfits to wear to big events or I'd look like the pauper I was.

Bennett nodded in understanding. "Well, your mother has her place here. She teaches yoga to the staff. I've switched her employee budget to our health plan."

"Very practical of you," I said. I hadn't intended any sarcasm, but my tone must have conveyed it, because Bennett stiffened.

He turned back to the door. His tone was harsh when he said, "Don't worry about Danika. She's like a part of our family now." The moment he was sufficiently close to the door, it opened and Adams stepped aside to let him in.

I wanted to say, "And I'm not," but I had done enough damage already.

Adams nodded at me as he closed the door.

Uggh. Disgust blasted through me as I trudged

around the wall back to the guesthouses. They could stay in their stupid estate. Nothing but bitterness and gloom there anyway.

But I felt a niggle of guilt. I had my own preconceived ideas about the Claremonts. And Bennett's treatment of my mother was proving me wrong.

Chapter Nine

By the day of the party, the estate was insane. Despite the early hour, I passed a half-dozen trucks as I left the stable to head to Mother's house. They were parked haphazardly between the barn and the back gate, florists and caterers and decorators.

The boxes disappeared from the studio. I had peeked inside, unable to help myself, wanting to know what Quinn ordered for his perky little instructor. I half expected tacky tennis ball centerpieces.

But tucked inside sparkly tissue paper were endless strings of beautiful fairy lights. I'd actually gone to the trouble to open one and plug it in. They twinkled softly in slow random pulses, like fireflies. I half wanted to steal one away for my room in New York.

It was going to be a beautiful night. A storm had blown the worst of the heat away yesterday, and we were enjoying a lull in the blistering summer weather. I took Jezebelle out each morning after Bennett was gone but before Quinn bothered to stir. Otherwise I kept to the studio and Mother's house, with occasional jaunts to downtown and Market Square.

The door squeaked as I entered the house, and I paused, hoping not to wake Mom too early. I couldn't hear anything, so I chucked my boots by the door and headed to the kitchen for the kale smoothies we'd made the night before.

I drank one with my nose wrinkled. But I had to counteract our cheese enchilada splurges or else I wouldn't fit in any of the costumes already being prepared for me for the next season. *La Traviata* in ballet looked to be challenging and different. I watched other ballet companies' interpretations of the opera while Mom slept in the afternoons, when the heat was unbearable.

In fact, I should probably get into the dance studio for an early workout. Riding a horse did engage my core and thighs, but I had a lot more muscles that needed attention. I was accustomed to working out and rehearsing eight to ten hours a day.

I pondered showering off the horse smell before going to the studio or just letting the sweat build up.

I settled on a quick rinse-off and headed out in a pale pink leotard with only the wispiest hint of a skirt. I tucked my toe shoes under my arm and ran lightly across the suffering grass, brown tipped and dry. Unlike its sister lawn inside the wall, where sprinklers kept everything lush and green through the heat, this grass was withering beneath the unrelenting sun.

I refused to draw any conclusions about my own life from this and insisted on holding on to the light feeling I often had in the mornings, particularly after a ride. I leaped over a low wall that bordered the path from the back gate to the dance studio.

No one had gifted me with keys to any of the buildings, but the studio had an entrance code, and I bent to tap that in. The door popped open with a satisfying click.

I breathed in the smell of the space. Floor polish. Window cleaner that kept the mirrors bright and shiny. Just a hint of a musty smell from the stacked mats. It had all changed so little from my childhood.

I kicked off the Crocs I was wearing over my ballet slippers and dropped the toe shoes on the floor. Instead of loading up any of my mother's classical CDs, I plugged in my phone and queued up some Nine Inch Nails. I wanted something edgy and dark as I warmed up.

The last ballet and the next one were both classics, but a recent production with my company had been a modern one set to a throbbing soundtrack. I had auditioned for a soloist position, and my ability to match the intensity of the music with less traditional movements was probably what got me a spot.

After twenty minutes at the barre, I began to do leaps to get warm. The room around me blurred and fell away entirely as I focused on the dance. I had not had the opportunity to join the most prestigious dance companies, as they had their own schools where you began your lessons as early as age six.

But I was trained well, and there were other opportunities for dancers if you were willing to take chances. My troupe was new but well funded, so far. I was learning a lot. It was a good fit for me since I had divorced myself from the ambitions of other ballerinas. I was okay with coasting.

"Came Back Haunted" came on and this was a perfect song for spins. I twisted and turned, feeling the rush of air against my face. I was the wind, a turbulent cyclone. Everything disappeared into my vortex. My mother's head scarves. Quinn and his tennis pro. Bennett's closed front door. Pearl's sneer. The cars. The grass. The wall. The wall. The wall.

The song ended. The playlist was over, so silence fell. I breathed rapidly, sucking air into my lungs. I had pushed hard.

Then I heard a sound. A clap. Then another. A series of them.

I turned to the door.

Quinn stood there, perfect in pressed khaki shorts and a crisp white shirt. He held a bouquet of flowers as wide around as a drum. His arms pinned them against his chest to free his hands to clap.

Now my chest was so tight, I couldn't breathe at all. I wanted to ask how long he had been there, how much he had seen, but I couldn't get in enough air to speak.

"Stunning," he said. "Just breathtaking."

My face flushed at the compliment. I'd heard these things a thousand times over from strangers, patrons, fans. But not Quinn.

"I'm sorry I haven't been to New York to see you," Quinn said. "Clearly I've missed out on something wonderful. I will remedy that."

My chest relaxed just enough to let me take in a normal breath. "Thank you," I said.

He came forward and extended the flowers. "These were always for you, but after that dance, they seem inadequate."

I couldn't imagine a bouquet this size being inadequate for anything. There must have been one hundred blooms in the bunch, tied together with multiple strings and wrapped in tissue and ribbon.

"They are beautiful," I said.

"They pale next to you," Quinn said. He was super close now. His shirt brushed the flowers, which I held to my chest.

We were separated only by a bouquet.

The scent of the blooms filled the space between us, fresh and sharp and achingly sweet.

"Why did you come with flowers?" I asked.

"I wanted to set some things right," he said. "The way I didn't write you. How I greeted you in front of the house when you arrived. And whatever I did wrong on our ride. I know I fumbled something. I'll probably do that a lot." His eyes were earnest, hazel and intense. He reached out a hand and lightly grazed my bare arm just below the shoulder.

Everything inside me blazed. It all mixed together. The dance, the dizziness, the intoxicating smell of flowers, and the man I'd always loved.

I had stared at those lips of his a thousand times over, since I was old enough to know about kisses and that I wanted him to do it. And I stared now, only moving back to his eyes when he shifted even closer, almost crushing the bouquet.

"Quinn, I—"

And it happened.

He leaned in and stopped my words with those

lips. His kiss was gentle, inquisitive, a question I didn't fully understand.

But I answered it. I'd silently compared every kiss in my life to this imagined one, but reality was so much better. He tasted like toast and coffee, slow languid mornings with just us two.

I kissed him back, my mouth parting for him, and he dragged me closer. I moved the flowers to one side and allowed him to draw me against him. Now I could smell laundry detergent and a hint of after-shave. His face was smooth and I let my free hand wander along his jaw, my fingers grazing his cheek.

We were here, after all these years, here.

His tongue sought mine and I met him with eagerness. All the moments I had dreamed of lined up but didn't compare to being here. I was lost, so lost, loving the feel of his chest against mine and his possessive hand pressing against my back to keep me close.

We lingered, neither pressing nor drawing back, just exploring, tasting, discovering this unknown part of who we had always been to each other. My eyes pricked with tears, remembering young Quinn, broken over his father, missing Mrs. B when she retired from the family. I had been there. Always.

We parted at last, gasping. Although our mouths

separated, our bodies stayed together. Quinn lingered near my face, his nose nudging my cheek near my ear. I closed my eyes and felt the warmth of him, the soft tickling of his skin as it shifted the loose tendrils of hair at my temple.

Every inch of me was alert and seeking him. My mind couldn't even comprehend that this was happening. It had been only a moment from my imagination until now.

"The party tonight," he whispered against my skin. "I want you there."

I tensed just a fraction, but he felt it.

"You don't want to come?" he asked.

I drew away to give myself some space. "Pearl said it was for your tennis instructor."

He shook his head. "I sent her away yesterday."

"Really? Why?"

Quinn took a step back. My body cooled quickly. I brought the bouquet back between us, holding it against my body in the crook of one arm.

"She was gold-digging," he said. His mouth turned down. "She wasn't even a qualified pro. Just an opportunist."

"Oh," I said. "Does that happen a lot?"

He ran his hands through his hair and gave me a sheepish expression. "I've been known to fall for it before."

I thought of the three engagements. He must be a target a lot. "I'm sorry," I said. "In our world, in ballet, there are also a lot of people who only want to know you for what you do, not who you are."

Quinn stepped close again and grasped my free hand. "You do understand! I knew you would." He drew me against his side, at an angle so he wouldn't squash the bouquet again. His hand pressed my head against his shoulder. "You're one of the few people in this world I trust all the way to the bone."

I flooded with happiness. He got it. He finally understood. I bit my lip to keep from blurting out how much I loved him, how I always had. I would tell him soon, but not yet. I couldn't scare him.

"You didn't cancel the party?" I asked.

"No," he said. "It's just a summer thing now. And I would love for you to be there."

"Are they still all fancy like they used to be?" I asked.

"Say the word and I'll require black tie," he said.

I laughed and lifted my head. "With only half a day's notice?"

"Anything for our Claremont ballerina." His finger lifted my chin so that I looked up at him. "I'm so glad you're back. I've been completely out of sorts since I saw you three days ago."

The little girl inside me soared. "I'll come to your party," I said.

"You'll be the guest of honor," he said. He stepped back and bowed. "And in honor of your prestigious presence, it will be themed A Night at the Ballet. Black tie required."

I laughed. "Quinn, you're crazy."

He shook his head. "Nah, everybody's always looking for an excuse to dust off their tuxes. Pray for the poor dry cleaners this afternoon, besieged by rush orders."

"I'll be there," I said.

Quinn backed away as if he was heading for the door, then abruptly he rushed forward for another stolen kiss. This one was different, eager, seeking, and full of promise.

When he let me go, he said, "I can't wait to see you. Shall I fetch you at your mother's house?"

I nodded. "That sounds perfect."

"Nine on the number," he said.

And with that, he turned and strode out of the studio.

When the door clicked behind him, I sank to the floor.

Had that just happened?

Had it really?

I leaped back up and pirouetted around the room. A party! A party! A party!

I was going to a Claremont party — as the guest of honor.

I couldn't wait to tell Mother.

Chapter Ten

8:45.

Mom sat in her chair, working on a new set of toe shoes for me. I told her I could sew them myself, but she insisted, cutting out the extra fabric and taking down the instep so it would fit my foot perfectly.

I made new shoes for every show. They broke down remarkably fast during the grueling rehearsal plus show season when I danced as much as ten hours a day. A dead shoe was torment if it happened in the middle of a performance. You were always safer getting a new one.

I paced the living room for the hundredth time. I'd been ready a while. Ballerinas did their own hair and makeup for shows, so once I kicked into preparation mode, I was ready within a half hour.

The dress I wore was sparkly sapphire, the

perfect color for my inky hair and pale skin. It made my dullish gray eyes seem to have some blue in them.

Two perilously thin straps held the dress in place. It floated over my body like water falling, ending in a flirty twirl of extra fabric that would flare out if I turned.

As someone who danced in front of large crowds wearing only a tutu and a bodice, I was not afraid of anyone seeing any part of me. The only other thing I wore was the barest jewel-blue panties, scarcely more than a thong. If I spun the dress hard enough, they would show. But I'd save it for a private moment.

My body tingled at the thought of it. This was going to happen with Quinn. I knew it. I'd seen his party nights a hundred times. The entrance. The greetings. Choosing a girl. Letting the party die down.

And then the stables. We'd dance there. Alone.

The horses and barn had been where we'd become friends. It was fitting.

I popped back into my bedroom to check my hair once more. I had gone full ballerina with an intricate tight knot of elaborate braids. Half my fantasy was having Quinn take them down.

I was getting it all.

I smudged my eye shadow a bit more. Stage makeup would have been too much for a party, even an evening one, so I had dropped it down a notch. No thick eyeliner. No fake eyelashes. But the effect was not subtle. I wanted to look as different as possible from that kid-friend Quinn used to know.

My body shivered and I wrapped my arms around my waist. The flowers Quinn brought me were all over the house in every vase we owned. A few that had gotten crushed during our kiss were pressed into one of my books.

I stepped away from the mirror and twirled in the dress. With a slow spin, I saw just a hint of knees and thigh. Big spin, yes, the barely there panties.

I was horrible.

I plopped on my bed and giggled. This was going to be the best night of my life.

Mom came to my doorway. "I'm worried," she said.

I turned from her disapproving face. "I'm a big girl," I said.

"But you have a blind eye when it comes to Quinn."

"Love is supposed to be blind." I felt like a chastised child, and my excited bubble was deflating.

"Only to the things that don't matter. Toilet seat placement. Big ears. Not fundamental personality flaws."

I didn't want to argue this. I stood up from the bed.

"Those shoes are bad for your foot form," Mom said.

I glanced down at the three-inch glossy black heels. She obviously hadn't seen the Louboutins, which were way worse. "I'll be fine," I said.

Mom pinched her lips together and fiddled with the end of her head scarf.

I crossed the room and brought her close. In the shoes, I towered over her. "I'm only here a month. It will be fine. I'll return to New York and he'll be back here and it won't matter any more than it did."

"I just hate to see you hurt," she said. "I always worried about living with people who had so much money. It twists things."

"Well, I'm a poor working girl," I said. "I went with fame over fortune."

"A ballerina's working life is short," Mom said. "Anything can end it. Injury. Serious illness." She hesitated. "Pregnancy."

So now we got to the real issue. "I don't think Quinn is following in his father's footsteps," I said. "He won't be marrying to knock up women and get rid of them."

"Of course not," Mom said. "That was flat-out

pathological. He only got away with it because of his money."

"Did you know him very well?" I asked. "Quinn's father?"

"Of course. He hired me."

"You think he screwed up his kids?"

Mom sighed. "We all do. Even if we try not to. Bennett seems all right. And Estelle was a good girl. Things are just different now. With money comes addiction and entitlement."

The sound of a knock on the front door startled us.

"Well, at least he's prompt," she said.

My heart hammered. It was time. I was going inside the walls.

I pictured walking beside Quinn through the gate and into the party. Or maybe we'd go around the front so he could enter through the French doors, as was his habit, at least back when I lived here before.

I took a deep breath and opened the door.

And sucked air right in again.

My mind felt erased.

It was...a carriage. A horse-drawn carriage covered in fairy lights and led by two mares I didn't recognize.

A man in a coat with tails opened the door to the carriage. "Your ride," he said. "Please watch your step."

I couldn't move.

"Good Lord," my mother said. I turned back to her. She stood in the doorway, her hand pressed to her chest.

I resisted an "I told you so," and took the driver's hand as I placed my foot carefully on the step leading up to the carriage.

"Don't lose a shoe," the man said with a wink.

"Let me know when it's almost midnight," I said.

I ducked inside the dark interior of the coach. When my eyes adjusted, I saw him sitting on one of the bench seats.

Quinn.

He was completely decked in a full tux, no jeans this time. His black jacket offset the crisp white shirt.

I could scarcely breathe.

"You are a vision," he said.

"You got a carriage!" I said.

"Well, a classic ballerina should have a classic entrance." He reached out his hand and I took it. "Sit next to me. Although, I have to admit, medieval transportation isn't particularly comfortable."

I sat on the cushioned bench. He was right. The seat was a little too high, and even though the uphol-stery was velvety soft, we both had to lean forward to avoid bumping our heads on the curved wall that led to the ceiling.

The driver closed the door and we were doused in darkness.

A white rectangle of light appeared. Quinn's phone.

"Not very period," he said.

I had to laugh. "It's perfect."

"I was planning this big ride around the estate," he said. "But now I think I might get a concussion."

I understood what he meant the moment the carriage lurched into motion. Both our heads cracked against the ornate carved trim above the bench.

"Ouch!" we said simultaneously and both bent over with laughter.

"We should take a shortcut, right?" Quinn asked.

"It's really about the entrance anyway," I said.

Quinn turned an antique latch that held the window closed and pushed the small glass pane open. He stuck his head through and called out, "To the party!"

A quick rap on the front wall signaled the driver's acknowledgment of the request.

Quinn ducked back inside. "So maybe I should have read the reviews on the carriage before I had one sent."

I kept a hand between my head and the curved roof. "No wonder everyone died on the Oregon Trail. They all had brain damage."

Quinn pushed down on the overly bouncy uphol-stery. Its springiness was definitely creating the prob-lem. "I think this answers the question about whether Cinderella and the prince got it on during the ride back to the castle."

"Quinn!"

"Well, I can't even make a move on you without cracking your skull." He leaned in as if we were going to kiss and another jolt of the carriage caused us to crash together, my forehead banging his nose.

"You okay?" he asked, trying to press his hand to my head but poking my eye instead.

I leaned away with a laugh. "Maybe we shouldn't sit too close!"

The carriage slowed and I peeked behind the curtain on the glass inset in the door.

We were at the back gate of the estate. Two boys in catering outfits were opening the double doors.

"We're riding all the way in?" I asked.

"I've always wanted to make an entrance like this," Quinn said.

"*Everyone* has dreamed of an entrance like this," I said.

He laughed, a sound I knew so well growing up that I would have recognized it if I heard it anywhere, in any situation.

We moved forward with another lurch, and

Quinn reached out to steady me. I held on to his strong arm. The sensation that I was living out a fantasy was so intense that I wanted to pinch myself. I was glad for the jostling carriage, as it was something not quite perfect that helped me stay in the moment.

Because all this was real. Really real.

When our movement settled down, I pushed back the curtain again. Through the thick glass, I could see the blurred glow of the fairy lights circling the patio and pool. Figures moved in the background, but I couldn't quite make them out.

I sat back. "Thank you," I said to Quinn. "It's unbelievable."

"It's not every day you have a ballerina at your party," he said. "You will be the belle of the ball."

As the carriage slowed to a stop, he leaned in and brushed a light kiss against my lips. Emotion welled up so hard that I could barely contain it.

"There," he said. "I managed to get one in without additional violence."

I had no voice to say anything. I just looked at him in the semi-dark, his eyes glittery and his nearness intoxicating.

The doors opened. All the party guests had come to see the carriage. Quinn stepped out first, then turned to me and held out his hand. I accepted it, and as I emerged, he announced, "I present to you Juliet Small, our very own Texas ballerina, here from New York."

Everyone clapped.

The scene was a vision. Over one hundred people in ball gowns and tuxedos, scattered beneath the strings of fairy lights. The pool was lit with dozens of floating flower lights that bobbed and drifted across the surface.

I stepped down carefully. Quinn lifted my arm as I moved closer, then turned me in a slow circle. My dress swirled around my knees. I knew it looked like a dark glittery waterfall in the light.

The crowd clapped again. I curtsied for them and Quinn drew me close.

I was here. It had happened. I was inside the wall.

And everyone was looking at me.

We wandered through the crowd. Quinn shook hands and said hello.

I was introduced to a more diverse group of people than I expected. There was a smattering of CEOs and bankers and stockbrokers. But I also met the art director of a cultural museum, two painters, a country singer, and a lot of couples who seemed to be just professionally wealthy.

We paused by an intricate cake with tiny globes of

light that pulsed throughout the dozens of tiny layers balanced on a spiral of small pedestals.

"It's like a dance," I said. "I've never seen anything like it."

"There's the lovely lady who created it," Quinn said, pointing to a petite woman in a classic deep brown dress and cowboy boots. "I flew her all the way from West Virginia because she's the best." He shrugged. "I also promised she could ride some of our famous horses."

He waved her over. "Jo Kagen, this is our guest of honor, Juliet Small."

If Jo was aware that the party had flipped themes only this morning, she hid it well. "Nice to meet you, Juliet," she said.

"You came all this way to make a cake?" I asked.

Jo leaned in. "Not often. But this guy here is pretty insistent on getting what he wants."

I could agree with that. "Have you been out to the barn? The blue mare is mine. Jezebelle."

"I haven't had a chance yet. I'm hoping to in the morning." Jo's attention was caught by a server. "Excuse me. There seems to be a cake emergency. Whatever that could be." She rolled her eyes.

She walked quickly away. I admired her creation another moment. Quinn definitely didn't leave his parties understated.

"You're amazing," Quinn said. "Do I get to dance with you now?"

"I've been waiting," I said.

He led me to the space in front of a small orchestra where a few others were swaying together to a slow waltz.

I hadn't danced with Quinn since his own Cotillion days, and that scarcely counted as he was twelve and I was nine.

Plus, he hated it.

We moved in time to the music. His dancing wasn't practiced, but he had confidence. He didn't exactly waltz, but held me close for a few steps, then spun me out. I was careful to keep the turns slow and easy, so my dress didn't get too much lift. Despite this one concern, our trip around the dance floor was magical and romantic.

The air was cool. The conversation around us was a low murmur. The music was divine. At the end of the number, we paused to clap. A waiter approached with glasses of white wine and Quinn took two, handing me one.

I drank very little, even at ballet functions in New York, as it was something that could sink the next day's rehearsals and put me at risk for injury. But I took a long drink for confidence. I could take it easy the next day. No Nine Inch Nails or wild spinning.

Quinn threaded his arm through mine and we headed back into the crowd.

I felt like I was floating. I glanced over at the wall where I used to sit. It was hard to see in the darkness, away from the party lights. But I knew the spot. I could almost picture myself there, perched low, watching with envy and melancholy.

A deep voice asked, "So which company do you dance with?"

I turned back to Quinn. He stood next to a dashing man with dark hair and arresting blue eyes. I assumed he had asked the question.

"Strativus Dance," I said. "We perform in New York, L.A., Montreal, and Paris."

"Impressive," he said and extended a hand. "I'm Ian Cooper. I'm regularly in L.A. I will try to come out to a show."

I shook his strong grip. "Thank you. I'd love that."

Quinn elbowed him. "Ian's a financial whiz. Bennett can't live without him."

"And there's your brother now," Ian said. He lifted his hand to his face as if he was going to straighten an invisible pair of glasses, then caught himself. He caught me watching and said, "Lasik. Can't get used to it."

Quinn looked like he was about to go to war, stiff

and angry. I followed his gaze, watching Bennett approach from across the patio.

So strange. They were never great friends, but there hadn't been any animosity between them. Although I guessed the woods had fairly crackled with their hostility on that trail ride.

"Hello, Ian," Bennett said pleasantly. Then with a curt nod, "Quinn."

"You showed up at the party," Quinn said. "That's new."

I looked between them with interest. Bennett hadn't been going to the parties? Why not? And why this one?

But when he turned to me, I knew why. His gaze slid down my body like an electric current, taking in each curve. My body responded, as liquid as the motion of my dress.

He cleared his throat. "Juliet, you look stunning. I heartily approve of a party in your honor."

The orchestra suddenly crescendoed into a rollicking foxtrot. It stole the attention of the party and several people whooped. Bennett turned to me. "Could I have this dance?"

Quinn cut in immediately. "She's spoken for."

"You had the last dance," he retorted.

"Ian already asked," Quinn said.

Ian's head swiveled to Quinn. "I did?"

I tried to hold in my annoyance. I wasn't a toy to be tossed around.

But before I could say anything, Quinn lifted my hand and placed it on Ian's. "Don't embarrass the lady," he said. "I'm going to pick up a bottle of wine for our walk. I do love a late-night drink on the loft in the barn, looking out over the fields." He winked at me.

My heart sped up and the previous moment was forgotten. I recalled all the times Quinn took a bottle of wine and a pair of glasses with him to the stable with his date.

This time it would be me.

Ian led me back to the space in front of the orchestra. I hoped he could dance to this. It wasn't exactly a number you could clutch and sway to. A few other couples were gamely two-stepping or just grasping hands and twisting.

"Do you dance?" I asked Ian as he placed his hand on my waist.

"Not normally," he said. "But I will make an exception for you." He smiled at me. "To make up for the brothers' bad behavior."

He launched directly into a perfect foxtrot, simple but well executed and easy to follow. After a few steps, I relaxed and let him lead me around the space. The other couples watched us, trying to imitate the steps. As we passed Bennett and Quinn, they abruptly parted and Quinn headed to the bar.

"What's gotten into them?" I asked Ian. Maybe he could fill me in on what had happened between the two brothers in the past six years.

He shrugged. "I'm not really familiar with Bennett's personal life. I live in California. I only come out when we are working on his investments." We made another half circle around the floor. "But I have a feeling it has to do with you."

I lost my step and we had to pause to get our footing again with the tricky dance. "Me?"

"Both of them look at you like wolves."

"What should I do?"

Ian smiled. "I think you'll handle it just fine."

The dance came to an end. "Thank you," I said. "You're a really great dancer."

He leaned in close. "Let's keep that just between us."

We walked back toward the patio. I didn't see Quinn anywhere. Had he meant for me to meet him at the barn? Is that what he had said before? I couldn't remember exactly how he phrased it.

Another man stopped Ian to ask him a question, and I stood by the buffet table, feeling unsure. A couple young women approached to gush over the fact that I was a ballerina, then moved on. Still no Quinn.

Then I felt a touch on my elbow. I sighed in relief and turned. But it wasn't Quinn.

It was Bennett.

"I think the next dance really does belong to me."

His voice was low and thick. A tremor ran through me. I didn't like it. I was here for Quinn. This dark attraction for Bennett didn't make any sense.

Yet, I was feeling it.

I didn't see any way to avoid the dance without being rude, so I nodded and took his hand.

The orchestra seemed to be waiting for his cue, as when we stepped out into the dance space, they began to play the final movement from *The Black Swan.*

I had never danced this ballet but I knew it well. The violins and flutes ran down the scale with clashing chords that struck me straight through the gut.

Bennett pulled me into his arms and we cut across the smooth patio floor in long powerful steps. His arms were strong and sure as we turned together, our feet moving in perfect synchronicity.

His hand on my back seemed to burn. We kept a proper dance distance for the tricky steps at first, then he crushed me in and we spun, tight and fierce. My leg between his thighs, stepping through, then around, as we moved.

I could not let my mind wander or I'd lose the rhythm of our dance. We moved like one person, tightly bound and headed on the same intense path.

He whipped me away from him and in the powerful spin, I felt the dress go high. When I came back around, face to face, I could see the hunger in his expression. He led us to the darker edges of the party where no one was watching, their focus to the inside and the light.

Then he spun me again, and again, and again. Each time he brought me back to him, we collided with more force, until finally he gripped me tight, crushed against his body. I breathed hard, unable to speak or swallow or do anything but look up into his heated expression.

Then he leaned down, his hands tight in their grip on mine, my body caught against him.

He was going to kiss me.

I panicked. I flung his hands away from me and took off in a dead run, sprinting for the back gate and the path to the barn.

I didn't know what I felt, but it wasn't right.

And it scared me.

Chapter Eleven

I paced the long corridor between the stalls in the barn. My anxious steps riled the horses, who stomped and whinnied along my path.

I paused in front of Jezebelle, hoping the sight of her would calm me. I held out my hand and she nuzzled my palm.

My breathing slowed finally. What had Bennett done to me? It must have been the music. Tchaikovsky was powerful and moving.

I pressed my cheek against Jezebelle's scruffy nose. Quinn would come out here when he realized I wasn't at the party. He'd know I had followed his instructions even if he originally planned to walk me out here himself.

I backed away from Jezebelle and paced the hall again. The shelf where Quinn placed the wine bottle with that other girl six years ago was as it had always been. Empty and waiting.

A few bits of straw strayed from the stalls here and there, and I absentmindedly kicked them back under the doors.

After another few minutes, I wondered if I should go back to the party. Maybe Quinn had seen me dance with Bennett and thought I left with him.

God.

I rushed to the stable door and peered out into the night. I could barely see the wall, much less beyond it.

What should I do?

I could climb the wall again. See what was happening.

I bent to slip off my shoes to walk out and do just that when I heard a sound at the opposite end of the barn.

My lungs drew in a long sigh. Surely it was Quinn. He had figured it out.

My heels clicked on the floor as I headed his way. The corridor wasn't particularly bright, softly illuminated for night. One narrow swath of light came from the partially open door of the feed room, which was one of the other entrances to the building.

A pair of black wingtips gleamed in that sharp triangle of light. And the cuffs of the sharp black tux.

I spotted the bottle of wine and the glasses and smiled.

But when the rest of him emerged from the darkness, it wasn't Quinn.

It was Bennett.

I took a step back. "What are you doing here?" My heart hammered.

"I wanted to apologize for frightening you off from our dance." He seemed to realize I was spooked because he didn't come any closer. "I have been accused of being too intense. I am sorry."

My shoulders relaxed. "*Black Swan* is an emotional piece."

"That it is." Bennett set one of the glasses on the shelf and poured a hefty amount of wine into the other.

Maybe I had overreacted out there. Probably to Bennett it was just a dance. I was the one all freaked out.

Bennett held the glass out to me.

"Oh, I don't know," I said. "I'm on a pretty strict regimen."

"I can respect that," Bennett said. He held the glass up to the light. "It's a good one, though, not from the party. My father was saving it for a big achievement that never came. He said it was his lucky bottle."

I moved closer to peer at it. "And you opened it tonight?"

"I did." He took a sip and let out a long sigh. "Now that was definitely worth waiting for." He turned the label to show me. "Twenty-four years old. Just like you, I believe."

"All right," I said. "You've convinced me."

He set his glass on the shelf and filled the second one. The dark red liquid swirled as he passed it to me. I took a deep sniff. It was succulent, woodsy and strong.

Bennett touched his glass to mine in a tender clink. "To our ballerina," he said softly.

"Thank you." That shivery feeling I was getting used to in his presence returned. I took a sip. The flavor was powerful and rich. "It's amazing," I said.

"Like I said, worth waiting for." His eyes said he wasn't talking about the wine.

His gaze was so piercing that I couldn't manage it. I moved away and walked along the corridor, looking at the horses. Where was Quinn?

I didn't dare ask, so I just kept going, pausing at each stall.

When I came to Bennett's stallion, I asked, "When did you get him? I can't remember. It seems like he's always been here."

"Lucky? A couple years before Jezebelle came."

"Was he a good racehorse? Did he win?"

"Not particularly. I think he has a few ribbons to his name, but didn't earn his keep. That's how we got him."

Lucky shuffled forward. "I'm sorry I don't have anything for you," I told the horse. He nickered in response.

"I love how you talk to them," Bennett said. He had moved closer.

"You don't?" I asked.

"Oh, the usual. Whoa. Giddyup."

"You say, 'Giddyup'?" I couldn't stop my giggle from bursting out.

"That's what they say in all the cowboy movies!"

This was true. But I'd never heard anyone on this estate say it. "Sawyer teaches you to make a little noise with your mouth."

Bennett leaned against the post between the stalls. "A noise? With your mouth?"

I blushed fiercely. "You know. Like this." I made the sound, a sort of "chick chick" noise made by sucking air through clenched teeth.

Lucky popped his head up in confusion. I ran my hand along his nose. "Just practicing," I said. "I guess anything works as long as it's consistent. A few of the trainers say, 'Come on.' It's really a combination of command and knees and reins."

"I could probably train him to go when I say 'Stop.'"

I shook my head at Bennett, but laughed anyway. "That would just be wrong."

He sipped his wine, grinning at me. "This is the most fun I've had all day."

I twirled my glass to watch the dark liquid swish around. More was gone than I remembered drinking. "You have to admit I made a killer entrance to the party."

"You did indeed," he said.

This would make an easy segue, so I took it. "Quinn arranged for the carriage. Do you know where he went?"

Bennett shifted a little. "Well, he's had to handle a little ... issue."

I withdrew my hand from Lucky and turned around. "What do you mean?"

"It's probably already hit the gossip sites. Such dirty business." He took another drink.

My stomach felt like lead. "Do you mean me? And Quinn?"

Bennett shook his head. "Oh, no. Even TMZ isn't that on the ball. His last fiancée. Apparently she's entered rehab over their 'toxic relationship.' Trying to rival the Bieber—Gomez thing, probably. She's an actress. All publicity is good publicity."

My stomach heaved. I racked my brains trying to remember when Quinn's last split happened. "Hasn't it been a few months?"

"More like a few weeks." Bennett stared into his glass.

I pressed my back against the stall door, trying to keep the world from listing sideways. "Is he going to go help her?"

"Not sure," Bennett said. "But he did get caught in a storm of paparazzi hanging out at the gate."

"Don't you have security or something?" I pictured Quinn going down in a heap of photographers, like football players on a fumble.

"Public road," he said.

I downed the glass of wine in a single gulp and handed Bennett the glass. "I have to help him!" I said.

Bennett took the glass. "Might want to steer clear of it for a while."

"Of course not!" I said. "He'll need someone to lean on. To talk to!"

Bennett laughed. "Okay, Juliet. Go rescue him."

I cursed my shoes as I dashed through the stable and out into the night. I was at the back gate in an instant, but the party was carrying on as if nothing had happened.

A few people reached out as if to stop me to talk, but I ignored them, frantically looking for Quinn.

He wasn't anywhere out on the patio.

I strode boldly to the French doors. I had only been inside the mansion a few times. Once, when I was four or so, I fell down and Amelia carried me to the sink to wash off my bloody knees. A couple other times I went in with Quinn when we were very small and Mrs. B brought me in from the rain to play.

Once Quinn was old enough to really argue with his father, we never went inside together again. He wanted to be out and away from the mansion.

But now, I jerked on the handle and went right inside.

Directly beyond the doors was a long room full of furniture and an elegant wood bar. A few older party guests lounged here, drinking and talking quietly. They all turned to look at me when I burst inside.

Quinn wasn't here.

From this room you could go straight through to the entrance foyer or off to the kitchen. I headed to the front, walking beneath the grand staircase with its gleaming curved banister.

A few men stood near the base of the stairs, smoking cigars. They stepped aside at my arrival and tucked the smoking ends away from me.

"Have you seen Quinn?" I asked them.

"He went flying out the front door a little while ago," one said. "Haven't seen him return."

"Thank you," I said. The front doors were formidable, twelve feet high at least. But before I could reach them, the butler appeared to pull one open. "Good evening, Miss Juliet," he said.

"Quinn is still out there?" I asked him.

"I believe so," he said.

I hurried through, out onto the porch where I'd first seen Quinn and Bennett when I arrived just a few days ago. It seemed like a lifetime already.

The circle was filled with cars. More were parked along the drive all the way to the gate.

A uniformed man approached. "Can I fetch your vehicle?" he asked.

"No, I came in a carriage," I said absently as I rushed by, ignoring his confused expression.

The walk to the gate was long, but I could hear the commotion out there long before I arrived. Headlights pierced the dark in every direction and the bright burst of camera flashes lit the scene at random.

Quinn stood at the gate with two men in uniform, waving his arms to shoo them away. When I got close enough, the flashes began popping like fireworks going off. Quinn hurried to me. "Juliet! You can't be out here!" he cried.

He seemed frantic and strung out. His bow tie was loose around his neck and his shirt was unbuttoned.

"Quinn, are you okay?" I asked.

"Not particularly," he said. "Let's get you back inside."

We hurried toward the mansion. "What's going on?" I asked him.

"Hell if I know. Apparently Margie — a friend of mine — checked into a celebrity rehab. The bloodsuckers showed up, hoping for a juicy headline. Shit. It's a mess." He raked his fingers through his sweaty disheveled locks.

"Just a friend," I said, not particularly hiding my disbelief.

"Well, she is now. We were engaged once."

"Thank you for being honest about that," I said, struggling to keep up with him.

"I'm going to have to go out to California. Straighten this out."

"Is she still — in love with you? Or what?" I couldn't imagine checking into rehab over a man.

"No, no, it's not like that."

We arrived at the porch. I stopped by the door.

"What's it like, then?" I knew I really had no claim on Quinn. He wasn't my boyfriend or even a lover. We'd barely kissed.

But we had just gotten started!

"She's fragile. Her self-esteem." Quinn stopped talking when Adams opened the door. He pulled on my arm. "Come on."

He led me inside and up the curving stairs. I hadn't been up them since elementary school. The playroom was still open back then, and Mrs. B was the nanny for the little girls.

We didn't turn to the left, where the nursery and children's bedrooms had been. Quinn led me right. I'd never been this direction at all.

We passed three doors spaced well apart. Then Quinn pushed open the last one. Inside was a huge room like a hotel suite. Fireplace, sofas, a small bar to one side. And other inside doors that led to a bathroom and a darkened bedroom. I could just make out the four posters.

My heart sped up. This was Quinn's space. His grown-up space.

He closed the door behind him. "I need a drink," he said.

His hands pulled the bow tie free of his shirt and he tossed it on the bar. Then he shrugged out of the jacket. "Too hot for black tie," he said. "What was I thinking?"

Of me, I thought, but didn't say it. I stood by the door, torn between helping him and fleeing this disaster.

He reached below the bar and brought two heavy tumblers to rest on the wood surface with a sharp clunk. I wanted to stop him from making one for me, but stayed silent. He dropped several blocks of ice into each glass and poured something amber from a crystal decanter.

I crossed the room and sat on a stool on my side of the bar. He pushed one of the glasses toward me. I picked it up.

He clinked his against mine, and I was reminded of the identical moment just a half hour ago with Bennett. But the feeling here was nothing like then. Quinn was frustrated and anxious. Bennett had talked softly, like he was wooing me.

"When will you leave?" I asked.

"Tonight." He glanced at this watch. "Well, in the morning."

My fingers tightened on the glass. "For how long?"

He tossed back the contents of his glass. "Hopefully just a day. Maybe two."

That wasn't too bad. A thin film of condensation had formed on my glass and I ran my finger down it, leaving a trail.

"Hey," Quinn said. He reached out and covered my hand with his. "Why don't you come with me?"

My heart fluttered. "Really?"

"Yes!" His face lit up. "We can make a vacation of it! See San Francisco. Eat on the pier!"

I pulled my hand away. "I can't. My mother has a cancer appointment. I haven't been there for her for any of her treatments. She's getting the results, and I need to be here this time."

His face drew into a frown. "Danika has cancer?"

I carefully checked my upset. Quinn had no reason to come in contact with Mother these days. Even if he saw her, he would probably take little notice of her appearance.

"Yes. Treatable. But I want to be here."

Quinn came around the bar. This time he took both my hands in his. "Jules, I'm so sorry. I had no idea."

I couldn't stop myself from blurting out, "Bennett did."

His chin dropped. "He's the better brother. Nobody doubts that."

"Of course not," I said. "Nobody is comparing you two."

He moved in very close until his face was just inches from mine. "I'm completely captivated by you, Juliet."

I could barely breathe. "Why?" I asked.

He tucked a loose tendril of hair behind my ear. "Because you aren't afraid of anything. You took off for New York and made something of yourself. And then you came right back, even though nobody here deserved another minute of your time."

"You do," I said.

He lifted my hand and pressed it to his cheek. "I do?"

He leaned even closer. I could feel the breath of his words on my lips.

I didn't answer, suspended, waiting for the coming kiss. I remembered the one in the studio and wanted another, and another. We didn't have to go to the barn, of course not. That was a silly thing he did when he was young. We were here, in his rooms.

He freed my hand from his chin and his lips lightly brushed against mine. But just as the kiss began to expand, a sharp knock on the door startled us both.

"Mr. Quinn, your brother has arranged for a car to take you to the private airport. Your flight leaves in less than an hour."

"What?" Quinn opened the door. "Now?"

Adams stood there in his formal butler attire. "He went to quite a lot of trouble since you mentioned you were anxious to leave straightaway."

Quinn looked back at me, then to the butler. "What else did he say?"

"That this would be the last opportunity to use

the company plane. He has business with it tomorrow."

I ran a finger along the rim of the cold glass. It didn't really matter to me now what decision Quinn made. He had baggage to deal with, and I was definitely in the way. I stepped down from the stool. "I'll let you pack," I said.

Quinn held out his hands. "Juliet, I—"

"Don't worry about it," I said quickly. "Thank you for a lovely party. The carriage was something I will never forget."

The butler disappeared from the doorway. Quinn took me into his arms again. "I will be back soon."

"I know," I said. "And I'll be here too."

He let out a long sigh. "Okay. Take care of your mother."

I stepped away. "I will."

The walk along the hall and down the stairs felt long. The crowd was thinning now.

Nobody looked up at me this time when I passed through. I wasn't sure if I should go out the front and around the wall or out the back and to the stable and around. Both seemed interminably long.

I paused in the foyer. Adams appeared again. "Your carriage awaits," he said, and opened the front door.

He was right. The valet stood by the open door,

gaping at it. He turned to look at me as if to say, "You weren't kidding!"

The driver was back up top. Quinn. He thought of everything.

I crossed the porch and stepped into the coach. Inside a small lamp glowed. No one else was inside. I sat on the bouncy cushion, then noticed a small box tied up with ribbon.

The driver closed the door. I held the box in my lap, not willing to open it just yet. That would be when the night would end.

The carriage jumped forward. I pictured Cinderella falling into the prince's lap with the jolt and wondered how anybody managed this mode of transportation with any level of grace.

The curtains were tied back this time, and I watched the mansion recede. The carriage went the long way around, down the drive for service vehicles, past the stable and the catering trucks, and then across the grass to my mother's house.

When we stopped, I picked up the box and waited for the door to open.

"Thank you," I said to the driver.

He took off his jaunty leather cap and bowed.

Only when I was safely inside the house did I sit on my bed with the gift. Mother was long asleep.

I pulled the sparkling blue ribbon off the box. I

didn't miss the fact that it matched my dress, as if Quinn had waited to see me to have it wrapped.

When I lifted the lid, I had to smile. Inside, tucked in tissue paper, was a soft ballet slipper made of silver fabric so sheer that you could see right through it to the stitching. Beneath it was a note.

On the side facing up, it said, "I have your other slipper. We'll have a proper fitting when the moment is right."

I kicked off my heels and slid the ballet slipper onto my foot. It fit perfectly, flexible and strong despite being so delicate.

I picked up the note and turned it over. And sucked in a breath. On the back was a name I hadn't expected.

Bennett.

Chapter Twelve

I had to know if Quinn was really gone. While passing the open gate the next afternoon, I spotted Amelia clearing dishes from a table on the back patio. I broke my self-imposed rule by marching right inside the wall.

She didn't blink an eye at my intrusion. "Miss Juliet! How was your party last night?"

"Lovely. Did Quinn actually leave on the plane?"

"I believe so. Usually I would have seen him by now."

"I see." I sank down onto a patio chair.

"I saw your carriage," she said as she stacked plates. "That Quinn is a rascal, isn't he?"

I wasn't sure if she meant a good rascal or a bad rascal. "It was quite the way to enter the party," I said.

She loaded the plates onto a tray. "Keep your head on straight around that one. He's a charmer for sure."

"I will." I hesitated. "Amelia?"

"Yes, child."

"Does Quinn...work?"

She laughed a little. "If he does, I don't know it. He's always here, doing something. Tennis or swimming or tapping away on a computer."

I seized on that. "Working from home, then?"

Amelia patted my shoulder. "Boys like Quinn do not need to work."

"But Bennett does."

She picked up the tray and balanced it on her hip. "Men like Bennett appreciate power. They do not easily enjoy the fruit of their labors."

I realized I was keeping her and stood to press a kiss against her pillowy cheek. "Thank you."

I hadn't told anyone about the slipper. But when I woke up that morning, my thoughts were definitely more about Bennett than Quinn. I shook that memory off and hurried back through the gate and to the studio door.

It was unlocked.

Mom must be there.

The door opened with a soft click. Inside, music swelled, a waltz.

"You're getting better than me," my mother said.

"Now sweep and turn and back to the step." She counted out the timing.

I slid along the wall of the entrance where the boxes had once been piled. Then I peeked around the corner. Mom was dancing.

With Bennett.

He crossed the floor in long bold steps. Mom looked small and dainty in his arms, the ties to her head scarf fluttering behind her.

Bennett wasn't casual, even on a Saturday afternoon. Pressed khakis and a button-down shirt. But a short-sleeved one. Probably his one concession to the weekend.

His arms were powerful, the arm muscles bulging when he turned Mom out and away from him. They were arresting, beautiful to watch. We must have looked like that last night. Until he spun me in the dress.

I remembered his hungry look and shivered all over again.

But with Mom, his expression was relaxed and easy.

The song came to its conclusion. Rather than hide, I stepped out and clapped, like Quinn had for me just the day before. "Lovely footwork!"

Mom pressed her hand to her chest. "I swear keeping me in shape like this is what's kept the cancer in check."

I swallowed at her mention of it. I could see she was tired. She said she would get better, as more time passed since her treatments.

"Why don't you take Juliet around the floor a few times?" Mom said. "Give the old woman here a break."

"You're not old!" both Bennett and I said at the same time.

Then "Jinx!"

My face grew hot. I had always called jinx with Quinn, but obviously it was something he had also done with his brother.

"You can tell we grew up together," Bennett said easily. Another waltz began. "May I have this dance?"

I set my toe shoes against the wall and kicked off the Crocs. I wasn't in a leotard today, just fitted shorts and a tank. But Bennett's hand on the small of my back was as hot and distracting as it had been the night before.

"Start with the basic step," Mother said as we began. "And another."

I moved with Bennett, learning the length of his stride, the angle of his body.

"Now outside roll," Mom said, "Promenade." She waited a few beats. "And back into the step."

We returned to the one-two-three.

"Now again," she said. "Outside roll, promenade."

Bennett and I moved with more confidence now. I felt the power in his step like last night.

"And HAIR-pin-now, ONE-two-three, MOST-ly good, TRY-a-gain." As the steps got trickier, Mom kept the count with her instructions.

We ran through the tricky hairpin syncopation and improved the second time.

"Now run her through what you know without my help," Mom said.

Bennett pulled me a little closer. His step between my feet was sure and his turn swept me along. His arms held me in place as we circled the studio.

I began to relax into the dance and let him lead without concern that he would falter. The music was easy and light. I kept my head tilted away in ballroom fashion, so we didn't make eye contact.

He spun me away and stepped through the move, picking me back up on the other side. He was good. But I knew that from last night.

"You get this from your dad?" I asked him.

"I don't think so," he said. "I never saw him dance."

"He did," Mom said. "When your older sister, Estelle, was little."

Both Bennett and I halted. "Really?" we both asked.

Then "Jinx."

This time we both laughed.

Mom stood up from the chair with difficulty. I could tell her muscles had tensed up quickly after the hard work. She moved to the barre to stretch.

"What did he dance?" I asked.

"Everything. But he had a particular fondness for the cha-cha," she said. She lowered carefully into a plié.

"Cha-cha?" I asked. That didn't sound very Claremont.

"The faster, the better," Mom said. "But he quit after the third Mrs. Claremont."

"My mother," Bennett said.

"Yes," Mom said. "She fought harder than the previous ones about the pre-nup. Sold things to get a lawyer. Went to jail violating the protective orders. Gave him a lot of grief. He lost his interest in lighter pursuits."

I turned to Bennett. "Do you talk to her now?"

"After what she cost the estate?" Bennett scoffed. "I've seen the ledgers."

"She's your mother!" I said.

"They all were mothers," Bennett said. "And they

sold their rights. They cared more about money than kids."

"Not Carrie," Mom said quietly. "She lost everything trying to get you."

"She shouldn't have signed the deal in the first place," Bennett said.

His voice was angry and his expression hard. But I could see the boy underneath. The one who wanted his mother.

"So you've never contacted her?" I asked. "You brought Rose's and Pearl's mothers back."

My mom shot me a look. I probably wasn't supposed to mention that I knew.

But Bennett didn't seem surprised. "Worthless, both of them. Did more harm than good."

Mother shifted away from the barre and back to the sound system. "We're losing our joy. I think a slow easy number would finish out this lesson beautifully," she said.

Bennett's face was still dark with anger. I wondered if anything could thaw that frozen heart of his.

The "Dreamcatcher Waltz" began. Mom could always pick just the right thing. After a piano introduction that brought to mind the tinkling of a music box, the violin wound a musical ribbon through the room, heart tugging, like a lonely child looking for his mother.

Bennett's jaw tightened, but he took my hand and resumed the ballroom position. He swept us into the steps.

For long minutes, he played it simple, the box steps and easy turns. But as it went on, the intensity of the music worked its magic. He moved with its rhythms, sliding along the sorrowful chords and turning me into its aching refrains.

The room spun past my vision, a blur of light and mirrors. I saw us briefly in the reflections, two people whirling through the room.

By the time the song came to its longing conclusion, we were both breathing hard. When it ended, the room fell silent.

Mom had left us alone.

"You dance like the music was made for you," Bennett said, his voice full of emotion.

"And you dance like you were made for music," I said.

He let go of me and cleared his throat. "It's a beautiful thing in its place."

I rubbed my arms, feeling a chill now that I had left his embrace. "It surprised you to learn your father loved it too," I said.

"We all know the family lore. The dancer my

father loved. The baby who took her from him and died anyway." Bennett shrugged. "I'm not my father."

"Thank goodness," I said. "He made a mess for all of you."

Bennett's eyes were hard as he stared straight at me. In that moment, I felt like business partners probably did when having to deal with him. Outsmarted. A little afraid.

Then he shook it off and straightened his already-impeccable shirt. His expression relaxed. "Thank you for the dance. Today and last night."

"I would dance with you anytime," I said. And I meant it. I worked with some of the most talented men in ballet, and I recognized a dancer's heart when I saw it. Bennett had it, even as he tried to deny it.

"You are just as talented as your mother," he said.

He watched me with eyes that made parts of me burn. I stepped to the barre to stretch, not wanting my muscles to get cold and tighten without a proper routine. And to escape him, just a little. He was so intense.

"I wish Mother could have gotten her chance on the stage," I said. "I don't think I'm as good as she could have been."

"I for one am glad she ended up here." His eyes caught mine in the mirror.

My throat tightened up again. I had to look away.

I was here for Quinn. He would be back soon, maybe even later today. Surely tomorrow.

"She has taught you well," I said. I laid my cheek against my knee, ankle on the barre, my face out to the room. Bennett still watched me.

That tendril of desire curled through me again. What was it about him? He could sear me with just a look.

"There's an exhibit in a small art gallery that might interest you," he said.

I lifted my head. "Really? Why?"

"It's an artist who took the works of Degas, the ballerina paintings, and rendered them in iron." Bennett moved to the barre, a few feet from me, and leaned against it.

I switched legs. "It does sound intriguing."

"I can get us in," he said. "If you'd like to see them."

I lifted my head. Quinn might get home soon. I wanted to be here. "When?"

"Whatever fits in your schedule."

I sat down to switch shoes. Bennett watched intently as I traded out the slippers and adjusted the toe shoes to my arch.

"When will Quinn be back?" I asked.

He didn't answer right away. I stole a look at him via the mirror. His jaw was set tight, his hand jammed into a pocket of his khakis.

"I can't spare the plane to fetch him until Tuesday," he said with measured calm. "It was promised to an associate."

"Oh." I failed to keep the disappointment from my voice. "He won't take a commercial airline?"

Bennett barked out a gruff laugh. "Hardly. He's completely spoiled."

The tension got thick again, so I continued to stretch on the floor. I pressed my forehead down and flexed my toes.

Bennett's shadow crossed me as he approached. Then he sat beside me. His voice was much lighter and easier as he said, "I'm sorry if that is a sore subject. I'll message Quinn and see if he would like a chartered flight. In the meantime, I'd love for you to come to the gallery tonight. Just as two people who appreciate dance."

I lifted my head. His face was calm now. "As friends, then?" I asked.

His expression didn't even flicker as he said, "Of course. I wouldn't ask anything else of you."

"All right, then. I'll come. Will you be sending a carriage?" I grinned at him foolishly.

His eyebrows lifted. "Anything for the Claremont ballerina."

I laughed. "Bring some big fancy car that will make me feel like a superstar."

"As you wish." He stood up. "Eight o'clock?"

"It's a date," I said. "Only it isn't."

Bennett nodded. "Fair enough." He started to walk away then stopped. "Can you indulge me in one thing?"

My heart skipped, but I said, "What is that?"

"There's that move — I have no idea what it is called." He hesitated. "Where the male dancer sort of spins a ballerina around on one toe."

I smiled. "I think I can manage that." I stood up and headed over to the box of powdered rosin in the corner of the studio to make my shoes slip proof on the polished wood floor. "It's called 'attitude derrière' and isn't so difficult."

"Now that's a name," Bennett said.

I flashed him a snide look. "There are a lot of funny ones in ballet." I ran through a few warm-up movements to make sure my muscles were prepared for en pointe.

Then I extended my arm. "You take my hand and walk in a circle. I will follow."

Bennett rose easily from the floor and held my fingers. "Like this?"

"Perfect," I said. Then I slowly lifted into my first en pointe for the day.

"I'm always amazed by this," he said. "I haven't seen it up close." He stared at my feet.

"I did it a lot right under your nose," I said. "You just didn't come in the studio."

"I should have been here every day," he said.

I swallowed over the lump in my throat. "Time for your walk."

As he began the circle, I lifted my left leg behind me in the correct position, knee slightly bent. His hand was warm and strong in mine.

He watched me, switching from looking directly at me to admiring us in the mirror. His steps were slow but sure as he circled me. His expression was awestruck.

Finally he let go. "I hope that wasn't too long," he said.

I laughed. "I work out, rehearse, and perform up to ten hours a day during the season," I said. "That was nothing."

"That's dedication," he said.

"It's required," I said.

"I won't keep you from your work," he said. "And I'm glad to know I'm not the only one with a seventy-hour-a-week habit."

My feet worked a small pattern to stay warm. "We're not the most well-rounded people, are we?"

He shook his head. "I'm glad to have found a fellow traveler," he said.

I paused in the dance. "Me too."

Bennett gave me a little salute. "Eight," he said.

I resumed the warm-up steps. "Eight," I agreed.

Then he was gone.

My mind wandered as I moved through the motions I knew by heart. So strange, the feelings Bennett stirred in me. But I could handle being his friend. He was right. We were both workaholics with a strong appreciation for dance. It was nice to find someone who understood.

Chapter Thirteen

My mother left to meet friends that evening, so when eight o'clock rolled around, I was home alone.

I never really had dates pick me up at Mother's house. What little I did in high school was out with girlfriends, occasionally meeting boys in burger joints or movie theaters. It had always felt weird to have anyone come for me at the estate, since it wasn't really my home.

Plus, our guesthouse was situated on a walking path, not a driving one, although Quinn had brought the carriage to my door. I wasn't sure what Bennett would do since you couldn't exactly drive a car anywhere near.

The doorbell rang promptly at eight. I took one last peek in the mirror. I wasn't sure how dressy this night would be. An art gallery could be anywhere on the spectrum from glitzy to ironic hipster. And an opening was different from just wandering in to take a look. One was fancy, the other acceptable in shorts and a T-shirt.

But this was Bennett. The man who wore khakis on Saturday. So I'd settled on a safe bet. A deep red halter dress with a lot of swing. It was short and flirty, barely catching mid-thigh. Since I could picture Bennett twirling me in public again, this time I played it safe and wore ruffled boy shorts beneath it. Too many people with too many cell phones out in the world.

My hair was up again, mainly because the cold front was long gone. The air was blistering hot and the parking situation downtown meant walking. I also slipped on ballet flats for the same reason. Wrecking my feet with heels was never a good idea if I wasn't sure how much I'd be in them. I got beat up enough in rehearsal.

Overall I looked rather unfortunately date-like. The main concession I'd made to the fact that this was a friends-only evening was the understated makeup. A little mascara. A light lip gloss.

The doorbell rang again.

Crap. I'd dawdled.

I hurried to the door, scooping up a tiny evening

bag on a long string. The door opened with a whoosh as I flung it wide.

Bennett stood there waiting. He wore a suit but the jacket was slung over his arm. A cool blue button-down shirt was open at the throat.

"Now that is an incredible dress," he said. He was about to say more when I interrupted him.

"Said one friend to another." I twisted the lock on Mother's door and stepped outside. "I do believe you might melt in the heat if you put that jacket on in a Texas summer."

"It's just a prop," he said. His grin was bigger than usual.

"I'm ready for you to wow me with your car," I said. "I want something straight out of *Fifty Shades of Grey*."

We began walking toward the front of the mansion. I figured he would park whatever he had brought out on the entrance circle.

"Funny you should mention that," he said.

I stopped walking. "You have a red room of pain?"

"A what?"

"From the book. His S&M room."

I could tell he was trying to stop himself from laughing. "I thought this was a friend date," he said.

My shoulder bumped against his arm. "Friends don't let friends have red rooms."

We turned the corner of the outer wall and I stopped dead in my tracks. "What the hell?"

"You said to wow you."

Sitting on the wide expanse of concrete that led up to the circle drive was ... a helicopter.

"Is this legal?"

"The pilot seems to think so."

"Holy crap!"

"I take it you're wowed?"

I snaked my arm through the crook of his elbow. "Yes! I am wowed!"

"Good," he said. "I'd say this is a successful start to the evening."

We approached the helicopter. A pilot in dark shades, a hat, and huge black headphones opened the door and motioned to the step. "Welcome," he said.

I climbed in and settled on the far seat. Another pair of headphones sat on the cushion.

"You'll want to put those on," Bennett said. "Otherwise the noise will be too loud for us to talk."

I slid the set over my ears. The pilot closed the door and moved to his seat.

Bennett pulled the straps across my front. When he snapped them into place, his hand brushed my bare thigh. My skin burned in a way that made me worry we weren't doing a great job at sticking to the friend script, but I hid my reaction.

He buckled himself in and put on his headset.

The pilot's voice came through. "We're ready," he said.

"Where will you park this thing downtown?" I asked him. I couldn't think of a single spot in San Antonio to touch down a helicopter other than the hospital helipad.

"There's a private landing pad on the top of the Amity Corp building. It's just a short walk to the gallery from there."

I wasn't familiar with that building, but I didn't ask, because the helicopter began whirring. With the headphones, it was just a dull roar in the background.

The butler Adams and Amelia came out on the porch to watch the takeoff. I waved at them. Amelia flapped her dish towel.

"This is so crazy for the short drive to the River Walk," I said. "I assume the gallery is along there somewhere?"

"I think I may have forgotten to mention the location of the gallery," Bennett said.

We lifted from the ground and I clutched my seat. The helicopter shimmied from side to side, then smoothed out as we shifted forward.

We angled away from downtown and headed north.

"We're going the wrong way!" I said.

"Not if we're going to Dallas," Bennett said.

"Wait! What?"

"The gallery is in downtown Dallas. I hope that's okay."

The sun was already dropping in the west as we flew over highways and subdivisions. "Sure," I said. "You're really pushing that wow, aren't you?"

"I'm trying."

The pilot cut in. "About ninety minutes," he said.

"Thank you," Bennett said. He reached between us and opened a small box on the floor. Inside was a bottle of red wine and two glasses.

"Another twenty-four-year-old bottle?" I asked.

"I picked this one up at the gas station," Bennett said.

"What?"

He swiftly cut the foil and plunged a corkscrew into the bottle. "It's a 2014 something-something."

I took the glasses out of the box. "Slumming it today?"

"I went to the corner store a half mile from home."

"You weren't kidding! Don't you have an entire wine room somewhere on the estate?"

"I was too lazy to find something."

"I don't think anyone on this planet would call you lazy."

He took one of the glasses from me, poured a generous amount, and handed it back. My eyes took in his expression as I sniffed the wine. I would need to take care, the way I was breaking my training lately, but a few sips wouldn't hurt.

I waited for Bennett to tuck the bottle away. He clinked his glass against mine.

This wine was simple compared to the one last night, but still quite good.

"Not bad for convenience-store wine," I said. "At least it didn't have a screw top."

Bennett sipped his and his brows drew together as he contemplated the quality. "I've had worse."

I wondered if picking up convenience-store wine was *his* concession to our friends-only night. I caught his eyes fixed on something and realized my dress was riding up. You could see the bottom of the ruffled shorts.

When his gaze lifted, that hungry look made my breath catch. I knew he was only playing my rules because that was all that I would allow. But if I gave in at all, even an inch, he'd be all over me. I could see his desire.

I gulped another mouthful of wine. "So how did you find out about this gallery?" I asked.

He sat back and surveyed his glass. "I own the building it is housed in. When I saw you again earlier this week, it made me think of it. I got an invitation to the opening weeks ago."

"It's tonight?" I asked. I was glad I had chosen the red dress.

"No, it already happened. I didn't go."

It would be nine-thirty at best before we got there. "It's open this late?"

His eyes met mine. "It is for us."

I took another sip of the wine, wondering if there was anything Bennett wanted that he didn't get.

The sun began to set, casting a gold glow over the flat plains of the uninhabited parts of Texas. Oil wells dotted the landscape, their lazy up-and-down motions breaking the stillness. We passed tanks, dairies, and herds of cattle. Clusters of houses in small towns and ribbons of narrow highways cut through acres of hay fields.

When we were silent a while, the pilot came on and pointed out the various towns and rivers. I finished my glass and held it loosely in my fingers. Partway through the ride, Bennett produced a luscious salad with a light dressing, fruit and seeds. "Amelia's suggestion, since I wasn't sure what a ballerina would eat, and I've been giving you ill-advised wine."

I laughed. "You can take me out for pepperoni pizza after," I said.

"I'd be delighted," he said.

The sky went black and we whirred beneath the stars, just pinpricks of light in the darkness. Eventually the horizon brightened as we approached the city.

"This has been a lovely flight," I said.

"If you decide you're too tired for the ride back, I have two suites at the hotel near the gallery," Bennett said. "Just let me know."

"Thank you." I couldn't imagine sleeping through a night like this, but it was nice that he'd thought of everything.

We approached a tall building with Amity Corp in bright red letters on the side. On the roof, a lighted helipad with painted lines grew closer as the pilot eased us down.

Bennett tucked the glasses and covered plates away in the box on the floor between us. I watched in fascination as we hovered over the roof, then touched down. The whine of the helicopter wings dropped out of hearing, then Bennett pulled his headset off.

My head rejoiced at being free of the equipment. I rubbed my ears.

"You all right?" Bennett asked.

"I am!" I said. I couldn't wait to get out and look out on the city.

The pilot jumped out ahead of us and opened the door.

The wind was fierce up on the top of the building. I was glad my hair was tied down, as it took both hands to manage my dress.

Bennett took my arm and led me to a small structure on the roof. Inside was a door to a set of stairs.

We went down a flight, then through a door to an actual floor of the building. Bennett punched the button for the elevator.

I smoothed down the tendrils of hair that had managed to escape my updo in the wind.

"Cute shorts," Bennett said.

My hands flew to my thighs, checking to make sure my dress was down. Sure enough, the back hem was caught on the ruffles. My face flamed.

"It's okay to say that to a friend, right?" he asked with a laugh.

I was saved by the dinging of the elevator. The steel doors slid open with a whisper.

Bennett leaned in close once we were on the elevator. I wondered wildly if he was going to kiss me here, but he only whispered, "If this wasn't a friendly date, I'd tell you how unbelievably sexy you look."

He straightened. "But it is. So I'm just going to say, love the boy shorts."

My pulse roared in my ears. I drew in a deep

breath so I didn't show how shaken I was by his nearness in the elevator, and all the trouble he'd gone to for this evening. My thoughts turned to the ballet slipper and his note.

I HAVE YOUR OTHER SLIPPER. WE'LL HAVE A PROPER fitting when the moment is right.

BUT THAT WAS BEFORE I HAD INSISTED WE WOULD be friends.

And of course, Quinn would be home soon.

It was better this way.

Chapter Fourteen

The temperature in Dallas wasn't quite as miserable as San Antonio, being a few hundred miles north. Bennett and I walked along the sidewalk past tall nondescript buildings set close to the street.

"Downtown Dallas doesn't have a lot of charm, does it?" I remarked as we crossed a street to another near-identical stretch of offices.

"There's a few attempts here and there, but I have to agree." Bennett gestured vaguely at the few scraggly trees attempting to grow in small spaces between the expanses of concrete.

"It's like New York without any of the urban grittiness," I said.

"There is no place that does inner city as well as New York," Bennett said. "Although I do like Tokyo."

I fell silent as I walked alongside him. Even

though I traveled with the dance company, I rarely got to set out and explore. The schedules were intense, ten-hour days at the studio while on the road. We could not afford to lose our edge by taking time off. Or risk injury with late nights or parties.

"It's just up ahead," Bennett said. "I can get a car for us for the way back if you are tired."

"For a few blocks?" I said. "Of course not." I lifted a foot and wiggled it. "Besides, I'm in friend-date shoes."

Bennett smiled and reached for my hand. He held it only a moment when he realized what he had done and let it go again.

I looked away, watching our distorted reflection in the windows as we walked. If we kept having to say it, possibly that meant it wasn't a friend date at all.

I tried to picture Quinn again and summon those feelings I'd nursed since I was a girl. They didn't quite spark. Come on, I thought. The carriage. The bouquet. The kiss! Don't forget the kiss!

When I felt sufficiently back on track, I turned back to Bennett. He glanced at his watch. "Our timing is good," he said.

He pointed at a door ahead. Two small elaborate lamps lit an antique oak entrance. Above it was a small pressed-tin sign that said simply, "Art Gallery."

In an open window was a sculpture in elaborate twists and turns of weathered iron.

The streets were quiet. All the other small shops and businesses with storefronts on this stretch were closed up and dark. It was almost ten o'clock.

"How did you get them to stay open for you?" I asked.

"I'm pretty convincing," Bennett said. "When I want something."

His pronouncement clearly had a double meaning. My heart hammered again as he opened the door.

Inside, the air-conditioning was like a cool breeze. A young woman in a silky gray blouse stood up from where she sat behind a long carved desk. "Hello, Mr. Claremont. Miss Small."

My eyebrows lifted that she knew my name.

The woman came forward with an outstretched hand. "I'm Tami, the art director here. I am pleased to show you around."

I shook her hand, then she moved to Bennett. I could see she was a bit flustered by him, but she hid it fairly well.

"I hear you are a ballerina," she said to me.

"Yes, my company is from New York," I said.

"How lovely. The sculptures here are based on the art of Degas. Where appropriate, we have placed a reproduction of the original art that inspired a piece near the new work."

She flipped on a light, and I sucked in a breath as the first sculpture appeared. The image was a ballerina in an arabesque. And the corresponding art was incredible, lively and three-dimensional.

"You can feel the movement," I said. "It's amazing."

The sculpture was primarily strips of iron, partially painted pale blue to match the costume of the ballerina in the Degas. The iron was bent and curved to show not so much the dancer herself, but the lines of her position.

"It's almost as if he knew the dance himself," I said.

"She," Tami corrected. "The artist is Blair Long. And she was trained as a ballerina, only to be sidelined with a serious injury before she got old enough to work in a company. Fifteen, I believe."

I approached the sculpture until I was close enough to touch it. "May I?" I asked.

Tami looked uncertain for a moment, then said, "Yes. It should be fine."

I ran my fingers along the cool metal. Blair had a gift. As I followed the fluidity of the lines, I could almost feel the iron bending. Without thinking about it, I moved into the position myself, arm outstretched, leg straight.

After a moment, I relaxed. Bennett stood holding his jacket, his eyes devouring me. I blushed, but it didn't take away from the awe of the moment. I felt the artist running through me, Degas, Blair Long, the dance.

"I assume there are more?" I asked.

"Yes," Tami said. "This way."

We walked around the false wall that served as the backdrop of the arabesque. Three more sculptures stood in a line, each lit from above.

In the paintings, the young girls were frozen mid-spin, arms outstretched. In the sculptures, they came alive, moving across the room.

I couldn't help but perform the turns myself. I wanted to laugh at the beauty of the sculptures, the movement they showed while being still. I whirled and whirled, exuberant in their presence, amazed beyond words at what this artist had done.

When I finally stopped, Tami and Bennett were watching me, Tami with amusement, and Bennett with that hungry look I had become used to.

"That was beautiful," Tami said.

I tucked a strand of hair that had come loose behind my ear. "I might have gotten carried away."

"No," Bennett said. "It was perfect."

His low voice sent another shiver through me.

"There are two more over here," Tami said. She led us beyond another false wall.

These sculptures were suspended from the ceiling, a ballerina in two stages of a grand jeté. "Ohh," I breathed. These were painted pure white. Their movement was perfect, glorious, inspiring.

I knew better than what I did next.

I knew a ballerina's body is her job.

I knew the movements a ballerina made are difficult and require care and precision and open space.

I knew each muscle needed to warm up and stretch and prepare for each and every position.

But I could not stop myself. Despite the small room, the intrusion of false walls and statues and little information stands, I took a couple preparatory steps and leaped into the air for my own grand jeté.

My hand brushed against a sculpture. I shifted my weight to move away from it, but my landing wasn't perfect. My ankle bent as I hit the slippery floor, and I overcorrected.

I vaguely registered Bennett's hoarse "Juliet!" Before I could fall all the way, he swooped me up.

The seconds ticked slowly as I felt each nuance of the movement. Bennett's arms behind my shoulders and beneath my knees. The twinge of my ankle as the weight forced it sideways. The hot bolt of fear as I realized I had fallen. And the soft thud of his jacket hitting the floor, dropped so that he could catch me.

Then everything returned to life speed.

Tami, asking if I was all right.

Bennett, cradling me against his body.

The room, suddenly hot.

My ankle, screaming.

My heart, thudding madly.

"Over here," Tami said, gesturing to a red leather sofa near the large desk. She picked up Bennett's jacket and laid it over the back.

Bennett carried me with long strides and set me on the cool cushions.

I took several calming breaths, then lifted my ankle, my fingers probing the tendons and bones.

"Do you have ice?" Bennett asked.

"In the back," Tami said and hurried away.

Bennett took his phone out and quickly tapped a few commands.

"Don't call an ambulance," I said. "They can do more harm than good."

"Just getting us a car," he said. "Where would you like to go?"

"It's nothing dramatic," I said. Now that the sirens in my head were starting to quiet, I could tell the ankle wasn't seriously hurt. I moved my foot back and forth. The pain was dying down to only a small twinge.

"What do you need?"

"Ice and pressure," I said. "I'll treat this like a sprain. It happens fairly often. Thankfully I'm not portraying a swan tonight."

Bennett gave me a rueful smile. "At least you can joke about it."

Tami returned with ice in a plastic bag and a hand towel. "Will this do?" she asked.

"Yes," I said. I wrapped the towel around the bag and pressed it to my ankle.

Bennett tapped out more on his phone.

"Will you be okay?" Tami asked. She looked positively panicked.

"It's fine," I said. "I shouldn't have been so impulsive."

Bennett stuck his phone in his pocket. "Car's here."

"Already?" I asked.

He bent down and scooped me up again.

"I can walk," I said, trying to hang on to the bag against my ankle.

"Not on my watch," he said.

Tami picked up his jacket and followed us to the front door. Outside, a gleaming black Mercedes idled by the curb. A driver in a gray suit hurriedly opened the back door when he saw us.

The deep cushions of the seat surrounded me as Bennett settled me into the car. He turned to take his jacket from Tami and murmured a few words to her. The driver closed my door and walked around so Bennett could enter on the street side.

In seconds, we were off. The streetlights came and went in a blur of white against the dark buildings. "Where are we going?" I asked.

"There's a twenty-four-hour pharmacy ahead," he said. "The pharmacist is meeting us with compression options."

We pulled up before a brightly lit CVS. A man in a white coat pushed through the exit and met us at the car. Bennett reached across me and opened my door.

There were no introductions. "I have cold packs that you can freeze," he said, passing them to Bennett. "And then two styles of compression wraps."

"We'll take them all," Bennett said. "Thank you for coming out."

"There's an all-night clinic about two miles from here," he said. "If she wants an X-ray. And of course, the hospital."

"Thank you," I said. "I don't think it is terrible."

"You can call around the sports injury therapists

Monday," he said. "It's a big city. There is bound to be someone who specializes in dance."

"I can report to my own trainer," I said. "Thank you."

He nodded and backed away from the car. The driver met him on the sidewalk, presumably to pay for things.

"Will these work?" Bennett asked.

I took a wrap from him and pulled off the packaging. "It will be fine," I said. "I don't even feel it right now."

Bennett's face was tight with concern as he watched me move the ice and slide the elastic wrap over my foot. Then I put the bag of ice on it again.

"Here, I'll hold it. You relax."

I let him take over and pressed my back against the seat. The exuberance of seeing the statues and the fear that I had injured myself had left me feeling exhausted and shaky.

But truly, we were probably overreacting. I had an ankle turn like this every few weeks, usually when I was paired with a new partner and learning his style on lifts.

I would wrap it for the next few days of workouts. And I would call Camille, the trainer, to make sure I was doing what was necessary for it.

It wasn't a disaster.

Bennett pressed the ice to my skin, his hand circling my ankle. He concentrated fiercely.

He cares, I realized. Bennett Claremont cares if my ankle is injured, if I am hurt.

His face turned to mine in the darkened car. He looked devastated now, as if he had personally destroyed my career.

I leaned forward and put my hand over his. "I'm fine, Bennett. It's just a turn. It happens."

His free hand moved to my face, tracing my jaw. All pretense about being just friends was gone. I could see everything there, his need, his concern, a dozen emotions. I almost wondered how many people saw this Bennett. The world was accustomed to his controlled mask.

The car slowed in front of an enormous hotel and pulled into the valet circle. Bennett glanced out the window. "We're here."

He took the bag off my ankle and added it to the pile of ice and wrap pads we had collected. "Don't you get out on your own," he warned as the valet opened my door.

Bennett slid away and headed out his own side. He stepped in front of the valet and reached for me.

"Really, Bennett, I don't need to be carried," I said.

But he ignored me, scooping me up in his strong arms again.

"This way," another man said, his gold badge pronouncing him to be the concierge.

I wanted to protest being carried through a hotel lobby for everyone to see, but we were whisked through a side door and led down a long hall.

At first I thought it was a staff entrance, but the hall was hushed and carpeted. In front of an elevator at the end, a uniformed man sat. "What floor?" he asked.

"Presidential," the concierge said to him and turned to us. "Enjoy your stay."

Inside the elevator were mirrored walls with soft lighting. The uniformed man turned a key and stepped out. "Let us know if you need anything, Mr. Claremont," he said.

When the doors closed, I asked, "Stay here often?"

Bennett shook his head. His face was still soft and concerned. "Just once before, a couple years ago."

"But he knew you."

"It's their job to know people staying in their suites. When I made a reservation, they let the staff know who would be in the private elevator. It's how they can make things secure without being obvious or asking for identification from people who might take offense at that."

"Would you?"

"Take offense? Of course not. I'm not Justin Bieber."

The elevator came to a stop.

"I really can walk," I said. "I'm bound to be getting heavy by now."

"Not on my watch," he said.

The elevator opened not to a hall, as I expected, but to a room. I glanced back at the panel inside. There were no floor numbers, only lit buttons that said "Presidential" and "Executive" and "Concierge" and "Spa."

"Do all hotels have this?" I asked. "A secret elevator only for rich people?"

Bennett laughed, the first time I'd seen the tension in his face break since my fall. He took me to a soft white sofa overlooking a bank of windows and set me down.

"No, only certain kinds of hotels have rooms like this."

On the side table were the items from the car. The ice and wraps. "What sorcery is this?" I asked.

"It's called excellent customer service and a really slow private elevator," he said.

The ice in the bag was melted and leaking onto

the towel. When I picked it up, Bennett said, "Let me get something else while the new ones get cold."

He headed off to a small bar on the right side of the suite, complete with stools and a sink and refrigerator. It reminded me of the inside of Quinn's room.

Quinn's kiss came back to me in a rush, along with the hope I had felt that more would happen that night. And then the interruption.

Quinn.

God, I was staying at a hotel with his brother!

"You said you booked two suites?" I asked.

"Yes, I have this entire floor," he said. "And the one below us."

I sat up straight. "You booked two floors of this hotel?"

"They weren't taken," he said. "They basically gave the second one to me."

He rummaged around in the fridge. "Oh good, they do have whisky rocks. This will do until the packs freeze."

"Whisky rocks?"

He returned to the sofa with what looked like two gray blocks in a bag. "You chill them to put in drinks you want to be cold but not watered down with melting ice."

"Crazy," I said. I rolled my ankle, testing it for

pain. Other than the discomfort of the cold on my skin, it seemed okay.

Bennett reached for my shoe. "May I?" he asked.

I nodded. He carefully slipped the ballet flat off and set it on the floor. "Might as well do the other," he said, and removed that one as well.

Now the other brother was undressing me!

Chapter Fifteen

Bennett set my other shoe on the floor, and I took that moment to scoot a little bit away.

He must have recognized my withdrawal, because he stood up and walked toward the bank of windows. "I can get a specialist here to look at you if you want," he said.

"I don't really think it's necessary," I said. My ankle was cold, so I moved the whisky rocks.

The Dallas skyline was lit behind Bennett, twinkling lights and the slow cross of an airplane headed for the airport. His pale shirt was stark against the night sky, and his pants were perfectly fitted.

Another tendril of interest unfurled in me, but I tamped it down. Wrong brother.

"I've only been to Dallas once," I said, rolling my

ankle and realizing it felt pretty fine now. I set it on the floor to test putting a little pressure on it.

"When was that?" he asked. He continued to stare out the window.

"Mom brought me here when I was about twelve, I think. She wanted to go to a dance exhibition of some friend of hers. Something with a lot of scarves and tambourine music."

"Did you like the city?"

I scooted forward on the sofa to exert a little more force on my ankle. It twinged slightly, so I backed off again.

"I didn't see a lot. A little dance studio. Eating burgers at some greasy diner. We didn't really explore. I asked to go to Six Flags and she said the roller coasters would destroy my spine."

Bennett laughed. "Mothers can be like that."

I sat with my back against the arm of the sofa and elevated the injured ankle on the back. RICE. Rest. Ice. Compression. Elevate. As I arranged my skirt to avoid showing too much thigh, I realized Bennett wasn't looking at the window but at my reflection in the glass.

"Bennett?"

The note of wistfulness in my voice put him on guard. I could see it in the way he squared his shoulders. He turned around and sat on an armchair near the window, a good distance from me.

"Juliet?" His voice was harder, almost a dare, as if he knew what I would ask.

"Why are you still so angry at your mother?"

His whole body became like granite, as if Medusa had changed him to stone. But I didn't care. I wanted to know what made this man into the ruthless person he had become.

Maybe I cared too. There were too many damaged things.

My ankle.

His heart.

"The five women who agreed to my father's ridiculous ploy to have children for money were selfish, vain, and heartless. They didn't even think about the babies they were relinquishing."

"I doubt that."

"You didn't meet Pearl's and Rose's mothers. God. What a crock. They jumped at the chance to get back on the estate. They had already gone through their cool two million and thought they could get more if the girls liked them."

"Did they? Rose and Pearl?"

"Of course. They got into clubs, drank, partied. There isn't a mother bone in either one of their bodies."

"They didn't have other children?"

"Rose's mother did. She ditched them with their father to get a chance at more Claremont money."

I sighed. How could I convince the man that mothers could be good when he had so much evidence to the contrary?

"My mother sacrificed her career to have me," I said. "She could have ended the pregnancy. She didn't know the dad very well, and he wasn't interested in me."

"Who was he?"

"Some flamenco dancer on tour. I met him once, when I was five. He was very strange. When I see his pictures now, I think my mother must have had very odd taste in men."

Bennett stifled a laugh. "Sorry, I'm just picturing a tall guy in a fitted pantsuit with hot pink stitching."

"You aren't that far off the mark." I relaxed against the arm of the sofa.

"Well, your mother is one of the good ones," Bennett said. "There's no doubting that."

"I really pray that her follow-up news is good," I said. My voice caught. The cancer just had to be gone.

"She's in good hands," Bennett said. "I chose the oncologist myself."

"You've been really good to her. I wish I had known to be here."

"This is what she wanted. The idea of you not dancing was the hardest thing for her."

"I can't stand to lose her," I said quietly. "I think that's what your father felt too. The fear of going through all that again."

Bennett's jaw got tense. I wanted to soothe him somehow. I dropped my legs to the floor and was about to stand up when he leaped from the chair. "No!" he said. "Your ankle!"

I had forgotten.

"I think it's all right," I said. "Maybe we can test it." I stood up on one leg, gingerly setting the other foot down.

His arm came around my waist. "Lean on me for balance. I don't want you falling on it again."

His body was warm and muscled. I wrapped my arm around him and lightly set my toe on the floor, then flattened my foot slowly and gradually.

My heel came down without pain, and I carefully, gently, shifted some weight to it.

I felt a small twinge, but it settled it quickly. Then I stood on both feet.

"It's okay," I said. "I think I'll be walking easily by tomorrow. I'll just warm up first."

"You want to stay here tonight, then? The helicopter is waiting either way."

I looked around the sumptuous room. I'd never seen anything like this. White rugs on a deep red-brown wood floor. Carved furniture and paintings that ran from floor to ceiling.

And the view. I moved as if to take a step toward the glass, but Bennett scooped me up again. "I can show you around. Walking is for tomorrow."

This time I relaxed into his embrace. It felt good to be carried, cared for. I folded my hands together in my lap rather than wrapping them around his neck.

"All right, pack mule. Show me around."

Bennett laughed and shifted me in his arms so I was more upright. My dress was too short in the back to cover me in this position, and I felt his hand on my thigh, holding me in place. Thank goodness for boy shorts.

We walked across the living room to the door closest to the elevator. "This is a bathroom," he said, bumping it open with his shoulder.

The light turned on automatically with the swing of the door. I gasped. This was no ordinary bathroom with a toilet and tub. An entire room opened up with a hot tub–sized bath in the center, raised on a platform with marble stairs leading up to it.

"Hell's bells," I said. "Now *that* is a place for a

bath."

"I'd be happy to serve as your personal assistant for one if you'd like," Bennett said.

I smacked his shoulder. "I bet."

"It would be good for your ankle. Contrast bath."

I realized I was feeling tempted by him. I could feel the muscles and hard planes of his body as we moved together. Desire unfurled in my belly.

"You'd better show me the other rooms before I take you up on that," I said.

His eyebrow quirked. "Friends only, of course."

"Of course."

His smile was infectious and I could only return it.

The bathroom had a second door and we moved through it. The light did not pop on for this room, so Bennett bumped a switch with his elbow.

My throat tightened. A bedroom. It was majestic, gold and cream, an enormous four-poster dominating the space. The bedspread gleamed.

"You'll like this," Bennett said. He took me straight to the bed and for a moment my heart skipped, imagining him laying me down on it and having his way with me.

But he left me sitting there and picked up a remote from the side table. With the press of a button, a large wooden chest at the end of the bed slid open and a flat-screen television rose from inside it.

I scurried to the edge of the bed. "How is this possible? The TV is taller than the box!"

"It's sunken into the floor," he said. "I was flummoxed by it myself last time I was here."

We peered together into the guts of the mechanism that lifted the television, grinning like kids.

"The stuff they put in hotels these days," I said.

"It's crazy," Bennett agreed. He turned the TV on. "I'm pretty sure there is a channel devoted to the arts," he said.

"You were watching an arts channel?" I asked. This was actually sort of charming, and a relief from picturing him on the gold bed with some other woman.

"I had it on in the background while I worked," he said. He flipped through the guide, then a classical concert with a full orchestra came on.

"They're playing *La Traviata*!" I said excitedly. "This is our next ballet."

He turned it up a few notches so we could catch the nuances of the music. I swung around on the bed to lie on my belly, watching the violinists racing along the beat of an up-tempo section.

Bennett watched me with a bemused expression. "It's a great opera."

"I've been studying it," I said. "It's one of those tragic stories."

"Yes," Bennett said. "I've always found it fascinating, all the different takes on the star-crossed love affair."

"They never figure it out, do they?" I asked. "The poor girl never gets the rich boy."

Bennett hesitates at my question. "Well, in this case, they find a way, but it is too late."

"Right. Consumption. Till death they did part. Everybody loves a tragic love affair."

I watched the conductor passionately wave his baton.

"Did you ever have one?" Bennett asked.

I tore my gaze from the screen to look at him. "Have one what?"

"A tragic love affair."

My cheeks warmed. "Not really."

He kicked off his shoes to sit more naturally on the bed. "What? The famous ballerina hasn't had an admirer sweep her off her feet?"

I kept my eyes on the television, unable to meet his gaze. "I found having relationships with other dancers was messy. And patrons were even worse." I shrugged. "So all casual. Nothing heartbreaking. Nothing tragic."

I didn't mention how none of them had been

Quinn.

The longing refrain moved from the full orchestra down to a few mournful instruments.

After a moment, I stole a glance at Bennett and could see the emotion on his face.

"I can see that you have had one," I said gently.

He shook himself, as if shedding a memory. "Yes and no. I was engaged. She left me for another man. Probably for the best."

I swung my legs around and sat up. This conversation wasn't about me at all. It was about him. "How is that for the best?"

"She didn't really want me. I thought she did. But she was like the others."

"After money?"

"Maybe. It wasn't me she wanted. Not in the end."

"What happened?"

Bennett unbuttoned his sleeves and rolled one of them up. "Nothing so tragic as dying of consumption. She moved on."

"Do you see her anymore?"

He moved on to the other sleeve. "She was around for a while. I quit going to our parties to avoid her. Quinn's parties, I guess."

"Is she still around?" I wanted to smack her smug little face.

"No," he said. "I think she's off in Florida now."

We sat for a moment, listening to the violins slide up and down the sorrowful notes. Our hands were just inches away on the gold bed, both sitting up, our bodies cast blue from the screen.

We breathed in time with the music, in time with each other. I thought of the various men in my life in New York. I'd tried, really tried, to open up to them and abolish Quinn. But the emotions I'd grown up with were tenacious. And the relationships felt so doomed. Even the young dancer I'd given up my virginity to could not hold me.

But this moment.

It was different.

I turned to Bennett and realized he wasn't watching the television, but me.

The colors flashed on his face. He didn't look so hard now, or so cold.

My hand crossed those bare inches and touched his. He didn't move at first, but looked down at our fingers. Every part of me longed to connect with him in some way.

His hand turned and took mine. A woman came onstage to sing with this portion of the music. The words were in Italian, but you could hear the sorrow in them, the regret.

Emotion overwhelmed me. So much sadness in the world. So hard for people to find each other and be loved. I gripped Bennett's hand more tightly, as if it were my tether to the world.

He reached for me and wrapped an arm around my waist, sliding me across the bed to rest against him.

Still, we only held hands by the barest of fingertips, watching the singer. She was arrestingly beautiful, dark hair, perfect eyebrows. When she sang, her face expressed the emotion with wonder and pain.

When the song finally came to its tragic conclusion, tears rolled down my face. Bennett lifted the remote and shut it off. The room darkened, lit only by the side lamps he'd turned on when we entered the room.

I wanted to say a lot of things. That this was how it felt to do ballet. That I was sorry for his heartbreak. And his father's.

When I looked at him, it was as if I was seeing him for the first time. He wasn't closed off, hardshelled. He was a Bennett I'd never known, not even as a girl. I'd never bothered to really try, always enchanted by the charming, effusive younger Claremont son.

My face turned up to him as his turned down. When our lips met, it was like two lost souls touching, realizing we were still afloat in a dark silent sea.

His kiss was soft and gentle, a caress.

My hand gripped his arm and another tear rolled down my cheek. What was this we were feeling?

I clutched him, leaning in, wanting to feel passion, wanting this to be more than a reaction to the opera. I needed this feeling to be real. To take me over.

But Bennett pulled away. "We do get overcome by music, don't we?" he said quietly. His hand rested against the braids in my hair.

He was right.

The party was *Black Swan*.

The waltz was "Dreamcatcher."

And now *La Traviata*.

"It's powerful stuff," I said. I let go of him and leaned away.

"I'll let you have this room," he said. "I'll head downstairs. Just call the Executive Suite if you need me."

The bed shifted as his weight left it. He scooped up his shoes and pointed to my ankle. "Don't walk on that," he said. "I mean it." He gave me a wicked grin. "I'll carry you to the toilet if I have to."

This made me smile, even though inside I was still roiling from the kiss and his withdrawal.

"As friends, right?"

He nodded. "As friends."

And with a quick wave, he was gone.

Chapter Sixteen

I drove Mother's aging Taurus to the medical center Monday morning, my guts churning for a million reasons.

For one, we would get the results of the PET scans to see if the cancer had responded to her treatments.

Second, Quinn should be back soon. By tomorrow, certainly. I wasn't sure how I would feel when I saw him.

But also, I hadn't seen Bennett since yesterday morning. We had landed the helicopter in a small airstrip south of San Antonio this time and driven back to the estate. My ankle was doing fine, although I had only done stretches and floor work since the fall, just in case.

"You're quiet," Mom said. "You going to tell me

what happened Saturday night or is it one of those things you can't tell your mother?"

I had avoided the topic the previous day, but now we were trapped in a car together.

"Bennett flew me to Dallas. We saw an exhibit of ballet sculptures. Which were amazing." I gripped the steering wheel. "It was late, so he booked a couple rooms in a nearby hotel and we flew back in the morning. That's it!"

"That's it," she said. Her fingers felt along the edge of her head scarf to make sure it was straight. "You sure have been quiet."

I reached out and squeezed her wrist. "I've been worried about today."

Mom waved her hand as if to swat away my concern. "I'm right as rain. You'll see. My hair is already coming back." She lifted part of the scarf to show me the fuzz on her head. "I just might join your dance company and steal your parts."

I smiled. "You do that. I could use a break."

"This IS your break!"

"Oh, right."

She shifted her purse on her lap. "But really, what is going on with you and Bennett? I left you waltzing together last week, and then you end up in Dallas."

"He just wanted me to see those sculptures. I

didn't even know they were in Dallas until he showed up with a helicopter."

"That's quite a date."

"It wasn't a date."

"Really? Flying to another city and spending the night isn't a date?"

I sighed. "I told you. We had separate rooms."

"Is this still about Quinn?"

We arrived at a red light. I didn't know what to say about that. "I don't think so. I don't know. It's so mixed up."

Mom reached over to me this time. "I think you're figuring it out. Bennett is a solid young man. There is so much more to him than most people get to see."

"Did you know his fiancée?"

Mother's face darkened. "Of course. She wasn't worth his time."

"What happened?"

"I'm not sure that it is my story to tell. As much as I want to." She sat back in her seat, hands on her purse. "You can ask your precious Quinn about it."

"What does he have to do with it?"

But Mother just looked out the window.

We arrived at the clinic and parked in the lot.

The staff was friendly and greeted Mother by name. We were ushered to a quiet waiting room.

Mom fidgeted with her purse, and I knew she was anxious. I could feel the steady drumbeat of my pulse in my throat.

When they called her name, she stood up and turned to me. "I know you want to be there. I know you do. But I would like to do this part of my journey on my own. Is that okay?"

I settled back on the chair. "Of course, Mom." I hadn't been with her for her diagnosis, or the chemotherapy. My mouth went dry. Maybe I didn't deserve to be here for this either.

She went back with the nurse. I flipped idly through a fashion magazine, emotions skittering around. Grief that she hadn't wanted me back there. Anger that she hadn't told me about her illness from the beginning. Annoyance at myself for not somehow knowing. Dismay that I hadn't contacted Amelia or someone close to find out what was going on.

We were both fiercely independent, I realized. I got this streak from her. A dancer had to be determined and strong. Once more I wished she had gotten her shot on the stage.

Stupid flamenco dancer.

The wait was interminably long. Patients came and went, some with hair, some without. Some with family, others with nursing aides. A few alone.

Mom had been one of those.

I was startled when Bennett entered through the door and sat in one corner. I waved at him. He didn't see me right away. Then he got up and moved to a chair next to me. He looked like he'd come straight out of a men's designer-suit catalog in a charcoal suit with a deep purple tie.

"What are you doing here?" I asked. I wondered wildly if he were also sick. If this was why he knew about the doctor.

"I'm usually here," he said. "I thought you'd be going to the room with her, so I delayed so I could get the news from you both."

"You—you've been here before?" I stammered.

"Not every time. But when Amelia couldn't make it."

"You?"

He smiled. "Yes, Juliet."

"But—you're busy!"

He sat back and crossed one ankle over his knee. "We're all busy. Your mother's busy getting well."

The door opened and Mother came out along with a male doctor in a white shirt and tie.

"Cancer free!" she said and leaned down to hug me. "Everything's clear!"

She let me go to wrap her arms around Bennett, who had stood up to greet her. "I'll be back to full dance power soon," she said.

"About time," he said. "We need to start the tango before I embarrass myself at a party."

Mother pressed her palms into both of his cheeks. "You'd never embarrass yourself anywhere."

The doctor shook Bennett's hand. "We'll have her back in three months for a follow-up," he said. "But everything came back looking good." He waved and headed back through the door.

"Thank you for coming, Bennett," Mother said.

"I wouldn't have missed this," he said. He nodded to me. "Back to the salt mines. Nice talking to you again, Juliet."

Then he was gone.

"I'm glad he came," Mother said.

I turned to her. "He brought you to chemo?"

She threaded her arm through mine to lead me toward the door. "A couple of times. Amelia came to two. My friend Bonnie to one. And Bennett, when he found out I had no one to bring me to a couple of them. I asked Adams to get me a taxi and the old coot tattled on me."

"Mom, I could have come."

We had just passed through the doors to the outside, and she stopped walking. "No, Juliet. That was not what I wanted. One of the greatest strengths I had when I started going through this was knowing you were out there dancing and living that dream. It was a powerful comfort."

There was no point arguing this, as it was over now. I opened her door. "I'm glad I got to be here for this," I said.

She sat on the seat and looked up at me, the scarf a bright spot of color against the dull interior. "I am too."

We sang goofy folk songs the entire way back to the estate. I parked over by the barn in the staff spots. Mom didn't need any help walking back to her house. The good report put some extra spring in her step.

Amelia spotted us through the gate and hurried out, hugging and kissing Mother at the news and dabbing her eyes with her dish towel.

We headed down the path to our house, but both stopped when we saw it.

The doorway was surrounded with flowers. Daisies, roses, carnations, baby's breath in a dozen lovely pastels.

A pretty wicker basket sat in front of the door. A card on the top read "For two strong beautiful dancers."

"Bring that inside," Mom said, gazing up at the arch of blooms. "That Bennett has outdone himself."

I picked up the heavy basket and set it on the

dining table inside. Mom unlatched the top and peered inside. "Oooh," she said as she unpacked. "That boy pays attention."

Inside were a number of gourmet foods. Dark chocolates, tiny wedges of fancy cheeses, fresh dark-green salads with hand-whisked dressings in clever little plastic shakers with chilled metal bases.

There were crystal glasses and bottles of antioxidant-rich pressed juice.

In a little white box was a breathtakingly lovely pale yellow scarf. A note on top said, "The last scarf." I recognized Bennett's handwriting.

Mom was right. I hadn't known him at all.

Chapter Seventeen

When Mom was fed and resting, I threw on a leotard and Crocs and snatched up my toe shoes. I would try some gentle foot work today and make sure my ankle was really okay.

But as I headed to the dance studio, I found myself walking alongside the wall to the back gate. When I should have turned down the path, instead I slipped inside the estate grounds.

The patio was quiet. I walked slowly, wondering if I dared knock on the back door. Or maybe I could go around to the front and ring the bell.

I could also head to the kitchen door, where Amelia would let me in.

But I didn't want Amelia.

I stood by an outdoor table, uncertain. This was

crazy. It was midafternoon on a Monday. Bennett wasn't here. Quinn wasn't here.

I was being ridiculous.

But the back door opened. Adams came outside, sharp and austere in his black pants and dark-gray shirt. "Miss Juliet," he said. "Mr. Bennett is expecting you."

"He is?"

"I'll take you to his office."

I followed the butler with his efficient stride. His hair, what little there was, was black and peppered with gray.

We passed through the back room, under the stairs, across the foyer, through a formal front room, and paused in front of a tall pair of ornate wood doors. I had never been in this part of the mansion.

Adams rapped sharply. When Bennett called out, "Come in," Adams opened the door for me.

"Have a good day," he said.

I clutched my toe shoes against my chest as I entered the room. Floor-to-ceiling shelves were lined with books. Bennett stood behind an enormous desk, easily as big as a dining room table set for eight.

The door closed behind us.

He looked different here, formal in his suit, surrounded by computer screens, ledgers, fancy pens, rich leather, and ornate wood.

"I feel like I'm in *The Godfather* and I've interrupted your daughter's wedding with business," I said.

Bennett laughed, and the relaxed expression revealed his dimple. Some of the tension left my body, and I could breathe again.

"I've been told I'm intimidating in here," he said. He came around the desk. "Let me get somewhere less imposing."

We sat on a chilly leather sofa, cooled by the air-conditioning blowing overhead. I kept looking around at the maps, the odd trinkets on the shelves picked up from travels. "Was this your father's office?"

"Yes," Bennett said. "I've never really changed it. It could probably use an overhaul."

I fiddled with my shoes on my lap. "You knew I was coming?"

"I guessed. Did your mother enjoy the lunch?"

I had trouble meeting his gaze, sitting so close to him. I couldn't help thinking about that night on the gold bed with *La Traviata* playing on the screen. "She did. The scarf — well, that was a lovely touch."

"May she never need one again," he said.

He grinned at me, and I was struck by how much more handsome he looked when he smiled, not so austere and chiseled. More real.

"I don't want to take your time," I said. "I really did want to thank you. Not just for the lunch and the flowers." I hesitated. "But for being there when I wasn't."

Bennett's eyes pierced me, not cold, but with knowing. I had wanted to be there. And I had not been given that chance.

"How about this," he said. "Now that we are better acquainted, I'll make sure you're kept in the loop. She has more checkups. If she doesn't let you know how things are going, I can keep you from worrying."

"Okay," I said. "Thank you."

"Just know she did it from her heart. She wanted you to be worry free."

"I know."

"She's a good mom."

"She is."

We sat there a little longer, and I said, "Well, I'm keeping you from your work." I held up the shoes. "I'm going to test my ankle out, just a little."

His face grew concerned. "You sure you don't want someone to come out and look at it?"

"I've been walking fine, and it's still wrapped. I've been through this before. I know the routine."

He nodded. "Okay. Buzz me if you need help. There's an intercom there that links to Adams."

"I remember. Quinn and I used to —" I faltered. "I've used it before."

Bennett still watched me, his eyes more intense now.

I was totally unprepared for what he said next.

"I wish I were my brother," he said.

"What?" I asked.

Now he looked away, eyes following the rows of books on the wall. "I've always disparaged my brother for his lack of direction, his inability to mature. But today I wish I were him. I can only hope he will grow up enough to deserve you."

My heart squeezed so tight, it felt like it had stopped.

Bennett stood up. "He'll be back tomorrow. The company plane is fetching him." He moved behind his desk, straightening papers. "I hear he is excellent company. Very fun. There will never be a dull moment."

I felt frozen on the sofa. I wanted that, right? Quinn was coming home.

But did that mean I had to leave Bennett completely?

"Will we see each other again?" I asked. I stood up and moved closer to the desk.

Bennett set down the papers and looked over at me with hope in his eyes. "I would like that."

"The dance company at the little theater on the River Walk always has a good show on weekends. Just local dancers."

"Should I get us tickets? You sure?" The warmth in his voice made me feel warm too.

"Yes," I said. "We do share this love of music and dance. It makes sense, right?"

He nodded. "I'll arrange it."

My chest relaxed. "Okay, Bennett. Take care."

I walked to the door, desperately wanting to look back at him, but not daring to do it. I tugged on the gold handle and managed to get it open.

Everything inside me was mixed up. Quinn. Bennett. Coming home. The dance.

But Quinn would be back tomorrow!

Chapter Eighteen

※

I didn't know what to wear.

Quinn would be back on the estate anytime now, and I had everything I owned out on the bed.

I picked up a sophisticated Yves St. Laurent sleeveless day dress with buttons down the front. It made me look like a posh New Yorker and had been given to me by a boutique to wear to a charity event.

Too much, maybe. But with the Louboutins, I would look a lot like I did when I arrived last week. A picture of New York fashion.

Was that what Quinn wanted?

There was also a light breezy sundress, sheer enough to give the illusion of being see-through even through it was lined. Sexy and summery.

Or I could go with the ballerina angle. One of my leotards from rehearsals for the modern show we had done had angular cutouts, making it edgy and hard to look away from. That would get his attention.

Of course, I could go traditional ballerina. Pale pink leotard and wispy skirt.

I fell back on the bed in my fuzzy robe. This was impossible.

Amelia was on watch for me, since Mother didn't want to hear about Quinn. She was in the studio doing yoga with the cleaning staff and horse trainers. I kept checking my phone, making sure Amelia hadn't sent me a message.

Finally I settled on a middle ground. A pale blue leotard with a long wraparound skirt, silky and sheer. Instead of my Crocs, I slipped on a pair of blue sandals. I could carry my toe shoes. Ballerina and pretty both.

I let my hair down, keeping only a single braided ring around my head. The rest was wavy and long. I hadn't shown my hair around Quinn since I was eighteen. And he wasn't of the mind to notice then.

Makeup was important to avoid looking like my teen self. I added understated smoky shadow and a lot of mascara. My lips were vivid pink to complement the blue top. And glossy, to catch his eye.

Now I just had to wait.

I wandered Mother's house. I still had three weeks here. Maybe if Quinn and I got established enough in that time, he would come see me in New York. We could travel together.

Or maybe this would be some short fling and it would end in disaster — bad enough that the brutal crush would be over.

My throat wanted to close up. Was that what I wanted? A broken heart?

I opened my empty suitcase to retrieve the photo I'd recovered from Mother's frame. Me and Quinn as kids. I wasn't in love with him then, too young for that, but he was still my everything. Best friend. Play-mate. I touched his youthful face in the image. The love for him flooded back at me.

A few days ago, Quinn had wanted to take me with him to California. I could only hope he was ready to see me again now. We hadn't exchanged phone numbers, so there had been no contact in these three long days.

My phone buzzed.

Amelia.

Car just pulled in.

I stuck the photo back in the luggage. I wasn't sure what to do. Wait to hear from him?

Of course not. I was going.

My feet flew as I left the house and hurried along the wall to the front of the estate. I realized too late I had left my toe shoes behind, but it didn't matter.

I was going to see him!

When I rounded the corner of the wall, Quinn was still by the car, waiting for Adams to take his bags out of the back.

My heart absolutely leaped at seeing him. He was super casual in jeans and a fitted T-shirt. But he looked perfect, absolutely resplendent in the afternoon sun.

"Quinn!" I called out as he headed up the steps.

He paused and turned to me. I waited by the wall.

"Jules!" He motioned for Adams to go on with his bags and came back down the steps. He held out his arms as we met in front of the mansion. "It feels like it's been forever."

"It has been," I said as I tucked into an embrace, my head on his chest. This felt right, totally right. I relaxed into him. "How did things go?"

He let go of me and led me to the side gate of the wall. "Well, the gossip sites got it wrong."

"Really? How?"

"Margie was just in therapy, not rehab. And I mean, who in Hollywood *isn't* in therapy?" He huffed a snorting sort of laugh. "It was fine."

"So she's okay?"

He punched in the code on the gate and opened the iron door. "Sure, sure. She was getting ready for another role. Some detective series. She's playing the red-lipped siren. It fits." This laugh was more natural.

He led us to the back patio and we sat on cushioned chairs at a table by the pool. The heat descended like a blanket. We watched the water sparkle for a few moments. I was content just to be there.

Quinn hit a button built into the center of the table at the base of the umbrella. One of the butler's boys came out.

"Can you set up the misting system for us?" Quinn asked.

The boy nodded and ran back inside.

He leaned on his elbows, his face in his hands. "Damn, it's way hotter here than in Cali."

I didn't know how to answer that. I sat primly on the chair. The pool lapped against the edges of the tiled sides.

"Hey," Quinn said. "Why don't we take a swim?"

I held out my hand and placed it on his arm. "Quinn."

My voice must have clued him in that something was amiss. His whole demeanor changed. "Oh, Juliet, I'm not paying a lick of attention to you. I'm sorry. I'm so distracted."

"I understand." My heart hammered as I work up

the nerve to say what I wanted next. But I did it. "Can you just kiss me already?"

His smile was what I'd seen so many times from up on the wall. Infectious and adorable and able to charm anybody.

"I should have done that first," he said.

He leaned in to me, his hand on my cheek, and pressed his lips to mine.

I sighed against his mouth. This felt right too. I was back on track. Quinn was here. We were together.

His lips moved over mine, gently, teasing, soft.

"You taste delicious," he said, his mouth so close to mine, I could feel the breath of his words. "Let's plan everything. Let's do it all."

My heart swelled. "Yes!" I said. "We can stroll along the River Walk. Go to the missions. Dance half the night." I remembered my ankle. "Okay, part of the night."

Quinn squeezed my hand. "I think I need to lay a little low for a while, on account of Margie and those rabid photographers," he said. "But we can do lots of things here."

"Of course," I said, tucking my disappointment away. "We can ride horses. And swim, like you said."

"Sounds perfect," Quinn said. He pressed the

button again. "I'm starving. Let me get us something to eat."

I waited with him for Amelia to come out, trying to set aside my discomfort at having our family friend wait on me. This is what I had wanted, of course. I needed to be happy that this day had arrived.

I forced myself not to glance back at the mansion. And definitely not to wonder if Bennett was working in his study inside it.

Chapter Nineteen

The horses' hooves thundered as we ran down the trail. My hair streamed behind me, and I hoped Quinn was noticing. We were headed to the field where we walked on my first day back.

We had a blanket and a picnic basket for lunch.

And I had some serious hope that things would kick up a notch.

The trail opened up at the grassy space and Quinn, who was just ahead of me, slowed his horse. I reined in Jezebelle and pulled up beside him.

"I probably jostled all the food," Quinn said. He looked behind him at the basket strapped down on his saddle.

"So it's shaken, not stirred," I said. "It'll still be good."

Quinn laughed as he dismounted. "You're a funny girl," he said. "I had forgotten that."

I swung my leg over and jumped down to the ground. The blanket was tied to my saddle in a roll. I worked with the string that held it in place while Quinn got the basket out.

It was Thursday, the third day since Quinn had come back. We'd been swimming and walking and hanging out on the patio. Quinn had gamely tried to teach me tennis, but I didn't have any aptitude for it at all.

He didn't tend to get up until after noon, so I spent the mornings dancing and making sure my ankle was healing properly.

He would kiss me and pull me close, but nothing else was happening. Every evening I would think, *this will be the one*, but it wasn't. I didn't know how to get us out of the friend zone.

The blanket came loose and Quinn took it from me, snapping it out over the grass with a sharp crack. The grass was tall, so we had to work it down, flattening a spot. When we settled on our rectangle of red plaid, we were hidden from the world, surrounded on all sides by the wild grass.

"This is cozy," Quinn said. "As long as the bugs don't carry us off."

I laughed and opened the basket. "Well, we have enough food in here to share."

Quinn laid back and stared up at the sky. I unloaded some water bottles first. I opened mine and took a long swig, watching him as he got lost in thought.

I was about to open another for him, then felt a bolt of courage and passed him mine.

He took it and sat up enough to take a drink. He didn't notice what I'd done. So I took the bottle back and drank again with a smile.

Quinn sat up the rest of the way and peered into the basket.

I recapped the bottle and sat cross-legged as he unloaded sandwiches. I would not be all crushed like a fourteen-year-old girl. It was just a water bottle. I leaned closer to him. I just wanted him to stop being busy for a minute. To look at me. We were at our spot!

His eyes were still on the basket. "Amelia sure packed a lot of things," he said.

I felt so discouraged that tears threatened to well up. I bit the inside of my lip and peered over his shoulder. "Looks good," I said. My face was inches from his.

He turned and gave me a light kiss. "This was a great idea."

That was better. Maybe after we ate, something would begin. Yesterday at the pool, Quinn had played with the string of my bathing suit as if he were considering something.

We just had to find the right moment.

We tucked into Amelia's lunch, deli sandwiches, fresh fruit, deviled eggs, and a delectable blueberry cobbler. When we'd shoved the remains back in the basket, Quinn lay back again. "This is seriously the life, isn't it?" he asked.

I curled up next to him, nosing in so my head was on his shoulder. I remembered the night that was like this when we were young, and my heart soared that we were back here. It's what I'd always wanted.

I nuzzled up against him and kissed his jaw. Sweat beaded around his temple. The heat was pretty intense midafternoon.

"Months until it will get any cooler," he said.

"We might be wearing too much," I said. If he didn't get *that*, then he was seriously thick.

He squeezed my shoulder but didn't move.

Now I sensed something really was wrong. I ran through the events of the past three days. Had I said something? Had someone else talked to him? Bennett? Had Quinn found out about Dallas?

I pulled away. "Quinn?"

"Yeah?" He still looked straight into the sky.

"Is something wrong?"

This shook him out of whatever he was thinking. He propped up on his elbows. "Things are good," he said. "This is good."

But it wasn't good. It wasn't anything.

"Did you talk to..." I hesitated. "Bennett?"

"My brother? Nah. We don't cross paths much."

I carefully released my held breath. "Was it your trip? Did everything really go okay in California?"

This got him, I could tell. He shifted uncomfortably. "I told you Margie wasn't in rehab. She got a new part. It's all good with her."

I chose my words carefully. "But is it all good with you?"

Quinn flashed me one of those disarming smiles, the kind that I now saw he used to deflect hard conversations. "My life is perfect." He leaned in and kissed the tip of my nose.

"Salty," he said with a laugh. "We need a dip." He got up. "Come on, lazy bones. Let's go for a swim."

He reached for my hands and lifted me up. I wanted to put a stop to this, make him stay. Maybe I should go for broke, tell him I loved him, that I couldn't stand this friendship. That I needed more.

I wanted to feel passionate about him, to get lost.

I just had to say it.

But Quinn had already let go and bent to retrieve

the basket. He wanted away from here. My fantasy in the field was not going to happen.

Quinn didn't want to talk about important things. He just wanted to play.

But I still had a few weeks to see this out. I had to hold on to hope.

Chapter Twenty

Mom watched the rain cascade down the windows and opened the drapes wider. A summer shower was always a blessing to the parched ground, but the air would be humid and unbearable for hours after.

"Looks like you won't be riding the trail today," she said.

I pulled on my boots anyway. "It's Texas. It'll stop before long. Besides, I doubt Quinn is up yet."

"That boy definitely gets his beauty sleep," she said.

"He's a night owl." I sat on a chair by the window, watching the rain.

"You been working out enough?" she asked. "You go right into rehearsals when you get back."

"I go in the mornings before Quinn gets up," I laughed. "And before you."

"I'm recovering from cancer," she said dryly. "What's his excuse?"

I turned away from her barbed remark, something outside the window catching my eye. A figure darted toward us in the rain, the butler boy. He didn't have an umbrella.

"Whatever is he doing?" Mom asked.

He knocked on the door.

Mom hurried to open it and let him inside from the rain. "Horatio, what are you doing here?"

He pulled an envelope out from under his shirt. "For Miss Juliet."

I stood up. Horatio passed me the packet. "From Mr. Bennett."

Mom's eyebrows shot up. I hadn't told her much of anything, but she knew I had been spending all my time with Quinn.

"Have a good day," Horatio said and ducked back out into the rain.

My finger slid under the flap.

Inside were two tickets to the Blue Theater. Not ballet, of course, the venue was too small. But a jazz dance. It should be fun.

Except.

Quinn.

How would he feel if I went somewhere with Bennett?

I sank back down on a chair. Mother paced the room around me. She always got agitated when it rained. She felt the humidity in her bones, she would say, part of the sacrifice of so much dance.

I held the tickets for a long moment, feeling uncertain. It was just a friendly date. We'd had several. Quinn would see that.

But I remembered what Ian said at the party. Both the brothers were looking at me like wolves.

Except Quinn wasn't looking at me like that now. He'd been so...friendly.

Relationships were work. Everyone said that. And Quinn and I had a lifetime's worth of history to build on. It was a solid foundation. We understood each other. Who we were. Where we came from.

The rest would come.

But not if Bennett was in the way.

I jumped to my feet.

"You're going to turn him down, aren't you?" Mother asked. She stood behind the sofa, hands pressed into the back. She had a scarlet scarf on today, bright as a poppy. She looked youthful, the hard angles of her thinness filling out again.

"I don't want to upset Quinn," I said. "I don't want to be part of a competition between them."

Mom came around the sofa and sat on the arm of

my chair. "You should know the truth about what happened between Bennett and Quinn."

My insides shook. "Are you going to tell me now?"

"I might. But it's not my story to tell. And I could see why Bennett and Quinn would keep it to themselves."

"Then don't," I said. "Just...don't. I have to see this out for myself."

Mother smoothed my hair. I had it up in braids in hopes we'd get to ride today. Her hand passed over the crown of my head. "All right, then. Go tell Bennett you can't go."

"I doubt he's here," I said.

"He just sent those tickets," Mom said. "He's here. He's waiting."

I looked out at the rain. "Okay."

"I have an umbrella in the closet," she said.

But I didn't listen. I opened the door and dashed out into the rain to the back gate that would lead me inside the walls.

I was soaked by the time I arrived at the patio door.

Adams spotted me and opened it to lead me inside.

I dripped all over the gleaming tile floor. "Sorry," I said.

"It's quite all right," he said. "Mr. Quinn has not come down yet. Would you like me to fetch him?"

"Actually, I'm here to see Bennett."

Adams's expression didn't even flicker. "Very good. He's in his study."

"I know the way."

The butler hesitated at that, but nodded anyway. "Very well."

I resisted the urge to shake myself like a dog to be a little less wet. I hurried through the foyer and the front room and stood before the big doors.

Today, one was propped open.

Bennett was at his desk, facing a side wall where a bank of screens scrolled with columns of numbers. He occasionally stopped the rolling figures and tapped something out.

I stepped inside the room. The rug was thick and padded, and I could feel the occasional drop of water running down my body to fall onto it.

He looked handsome and determined, leaning into his work. His jacket was draped over the sofa, so he wore only a custom-fitted dress shirt, no tie.

Maybe I shouldn't interrupt him. I took a couple more steps forward to set the tickets on the end table by the sofa, but this movement caught his attention. He swiveled in his chair.

"Juliet. You're here."

I held up the envelope. "I brought these."

"The tickets?"

"I can't go," I said quickly.

Bennett stood up, and I took a step back.

"Is your mother okay?" he asked.

"She's fine."

He came around the desk and moved behind me to close the door.

His nearness was like a drug. I instantly felt different. Anxious. Vibrating with energy. I took another step away.

"Is this about Quinn?" he asked.

"No," I said, then, "Yes."

"But this dance performance was just for two people who love music and dance. That's what you said." He sat on the sofa.

I relaxed now that he wasn't towering over me. "I know. But I just... I don't know."

"Come sit here," he said.

I didn't mean to comply, but I did. I sat on the sofa next to him.

He took my hand. "I know you love Quinn. I know you always have."

I couldn't swallow over the lump in my throat. I nodded.

"He seems pretty taken with you."

My gaze flickered down.

He squeezed my fingers. "Is all that okay?"

"Of course," I said with a false laugh. "You know Quinn. He's always been the charmer."

"He has."

We sat there another moment, inches from each other. That tension curled in me again. I discovered that I wanted to be closer to him. I wanted his hands on me.

Think of Quinn, I told myself.

I searched for something to say. "I listened to *La Traviata* again yesterday," I said. "I'm trying to really learn it."

"So did I," he said quietly.

"Really?"

"It's my favorite now." His eyes wouldn't leave my face. "It will always make me think of you."

Bennett's throat worked as he swallowed. He was feeling something too.

"So, with the tickets, are you saying good-bye?" he asked.

"I'm not leaving for another two weeks," I said.

"But you're saying good-bye to me." His voice was insistent.

"I will have to go no matter what," I said. "*La Traviata* is waiting."

"The tragic love story."

I didn't know what he was trying to say. "It's just a ballet."

"But you're going back to New York," he said. "Quinn or no Quinn?"

"Yes." Why did he keep asking this?

Now his voice was a growl. "Then I have nothing to lose."

Before I could ask what he meant, his lips crushed against mine.

This was unlike any kiss I had experienced with him or any other man, demanding, passionate, urgent. I couldn't think. I couldn't breathe. My body sparked in a thousand places, pressing against him, wanting to be possessed.

His mouth took mine hungrily, and his strong arms pulled me against him until I sat partially on his lap. I could feel him with every inch of my body, his hard chest, the muscular thighs. And between us, how much he desired me, hot against my leg.

I broke away, gasping, unsure. What did I really want? It had always been Quinn. But I wasn't certain anymore. How could I feel this way with Bennett if I loved Quinn?

His hands held either side of my face, and his eyes bored into mine. "Are you saying no? I will walk away if you are really saying no."

My gaze locked on his. The look there was frightening, exciting, and hungry. My eyes fell back to his lips and that was all he needed for an answer as he pressed into my mouth again. This time he sought more, parting my lips, his tongue finding mine.

Time ceased to exist. I fell into the kiss, my hands moving to his neck, tangling into the curls at the base of his head. I'd made Quinn kiss me again, and I'd worked hard to feel something. But it was hollow, empty, nothing like this. Nothing at all.

Bennett's hands grasped the waistband of my jeans. His grip was possessive, primal, unrelenting. He was not going to let me go.

I didn't want him to.

My body moved into him, my tongue seeking his. One of his hands roamed up my rib cage, exploring each curve. It rested at the bottom of my breast where the tight tank top hugged my body like a second skin.

His thumb flicked upward, catching the nipple. I sucked in a breath against his mouth. Everything burned. His mouth moved to my jaw, my neck, just below my ear. His hand shifted under my shirt. His warm skin possessed the naked breast, and I arched against him.

I was supposed to be breaking away from Bennett, but I was falling into him instead.

He pushed the shirt out of his way and his mouth

descended on a puckered nipple. I cried out, clutching his hair. Tears sparked in my eyes as emotion flooded me, more than just desire. I wanted this. I had wanted this all along.

My body moved into him, rocking against the erection. He released me and pressed me down on the sofa.

I remembered seeing the gold sheets in the hotel in Dallas, and how I'd pictured us there. It must have been there all along, this need of him. He'd found a way to get to me, get me past Quinn.

Quinn.

He was somewhere in the house.

But Bennett's mouth settled on my breast again as my shirt moved out of his way. His hand worked on the button to my jeans, and my mind was erased of anything but how I felt.

The air cooled the skin of my belly as my jeans moved down. They were only to my knees when Bennett's fingers slid inside my panties, his thumb caressing me. I arched again and grasped his shoulders, utterly lost in sensation.

Lightning sparks of pleasure bolted through me from belly to breast. I writhed beneath his touch, then my nipple cooled as his head began to move down.

He feathered kisses along my ribs, across my

navel, and down to where he'd shoved my panties aside. When his warm mouth reached its destination, my hips rose to meet him.

I was lost, completely lost, unable to think of anything but his hot seeking tongue and the ripples coursing through me. He was patient and attentive, alternately bold and gentle. I moved up and up into the need of him, my hands on the sofa, clutching the cushions.

He sucked against the throbbing nub and I went over the edge, my body pulsing against him. I cried out, my hands moving to his head, the powerful waves of orgasm wiping out anything but Bennett.

He brought me down gently with soft nipping kisses. My head fell back on the cool leather, emotionally spent, overwrought.

Bennett. Quinn. Bennett. Quinn. What was I doing?

I wanted more of him. I wanted to see him, touch him, taste every part of him.

But this wasn't what was supposed to happen. An unexpected whimpering sound escaped my throat.

Bennett heard me and backed away. "I'm sorry, Juliet. I pushed. God." He ran his hands through his dark hair. "Shit." He walked to the other side of the room.

I didn't move. I knew I was all exposed, my shirt

to my neck and my jeans to my knees. But I couldn't do anything. I had to pull myself together. Bennett was blaming himself for something that wasn't his fault. It was me. I couldn't figure out what I wanted. My head and my body were not agreeing.

I had to figure out my heart.

After three deep calming breaths, I managed to sit up, straighten my shirt, and stand.

As I buttoned my jeans, I said, "Bennett, it's okay. I'm just sort of...lost right now."

I looked around the dim room. Bennett's monitors had gone into hibernation. The dark skies persisted, the rain falling down the panes.

But Bennett was gone.

Chapter Twenty-One

I smoothed back my hair. Walk of shame, indeed.

I pushed open the heavy door to Bennett's study. Outside, the formal room was empty. I crossed it quickly and walked to the front foyer.

"Juliet?"

I looked up the curving staircase.

It was Quinn, still in his bathrobe.

"You're up early," he said.

"It's almost noon," I said.

He came down the stairs slowly, assessing me. "You came in the house on your own. You don't normally do that." He paused on the last step, looking through the formal room to the cocked door of Bennett's study. "Did you come to see my brother?"

He took in my wild hair, the strands coming out of the braids. "What did he do to you?" He lifted his hand to touch them, but I flinched.

His hand came down. "Did you fall for him?"

I shook my head. "No, that's not how it is."

Quinn's face was dark. "He's ruthless, Juliet. Do you know what business partners call him?"

I shook my head.

"Sonbitch Bennett."

I wanted away from this conversation. I needed to think. To sort everything out.

But Quinn moved closer. "I didn't want to tell you this, but when I got to California, the photographers followed me there." He jerked on the ties of his robe. "It's like they knew. Like they were tipped off."

He looked right into my eyes. "I was on a private plane, Jules. How would they know unless somebody told them?"

Quinn paced a few steps. "And I never understood why those photographers were here the night of the party. That's never happened, not all these years, no matter what I was into, who I was seeing. Why this time?"

He whipped around to me. I wrapped my arms around my waist.

"Did he make a move on you that night? And

while I was gone?" He came over to me and grasped both arms. "Did he?"

I didn't answer, shocked silent.

"He did!" Quinn let me go. "That son of a bitch! This is about Pamela. I know it."

"Who's Pamela?" I asked.

Quinn took my arm and led me across the foyer to the side opposite Bennett's study. We entered a small drawing room with a couple of chairs. He closed the door. "She was his fiancée. He didn't take care of her. She wasn't into it. It just happened."

"What happened?"

Quinn raked his hair. "She and I had a thing."

I took a step away from him. "A thing?"

He reached out for me. "It wasn't a big thing. Just a thing."

"You slept with her?" My voice was raspy with shock.

"He wasn't right for her," Quinn insisted.

"And you were?" So this is what my mother knew. The story that wasn't hers to tell. The heat rose in me then. I couldn't take this. Not one more minute of this.

I jerked open the door to the room and dashed into the foyer. None of this was right. None of it.

I ran straight for the front entrance, and for once

Adams wasn't instantly there. I pulled on the heavy door and ran out into the rain.

I didn't want any of this. Not at all.

I would not go inside these walls again.

Chapter Twenty-Two

✿

Mom didn't say a word when I ran past her straight to my room.

I stripped out of the wet jeans and tank. I jerked my hair from the half-wrecked braids and threw on a robe.

Only when I was in a hot shower did I start to calm down.

God.

Bennett's fiancée. And Quinn.

Had Bennett really seduced me just to get back at his brother?

What sort of people were they?

I shampooed my hair. There was only one solution to what was going on here.

I had to leave.

Mom was doing fine. She'd come see me when *La Traviata* came out.

I could use some free days in the city. Visit the new World Trade Center. Eat a hot dog in Central Park and walk it off.

Yes, this was the answer.

I would go back to New York.

I shut off the spray. Despite my resolve, the idea of not seeing Bennett again threatened to wreck me. But nothing that had happened between us was true. It was just a revenge plot, and I was the murder weapon. Bennett saw that Quinn wanted me. He took me instead.

God.

"Mom?" I called out, wrapping myself up in a white robe.

She was at the door when I opened it. "You okay, Juliet?" Concern etched her face. I swallowed at the poppy scarf, wondering if Bennett had bought it for her too. At least that part of him, the things he did before I came, were real.

"Can you look up flights to New York? See if there is anything I can do today?"

"Today? You're leaving today?"

I could see she thought I was overreacting. "I have to get out of here, Mom," I said. "I have to."

She pulled me into her and rested my head on her

shoulder. "I take it things did not go well with Bennett," she said.

I shook my head against her neck.

"You sure running is the way to go? Sometimes facing our problems is the best."

I shook my head again.

"I'll tell you what," she said. "I'll get you a ticket for today, and then I'll come out in a week or two. We can still spend some of your break together."

I pulled back. "You feeling up to traveling?"

"I'm getting better every day right now. I think I'll be up for it."

"Okay," I said.

She patted my hand. "I'll get it all arranged."

Mom headed back to the living room. I turned to the half-fogged mirror. My hair was in chaotic wet strands. I set to combing it out.

I could still feel Bennett on my body, his hands, his mouth. I gripped the comb. This was wrong. All of it. I had to get away from both brothers. I was free of Quinn now. I would find someone. It would work. I had shaken loose from my childhood.

I'd done what I'd set out to do.

Once my hair was straight and up in a tight knot at my neck, I headed to my room. Traveling clothes. Something simple. Jeans and a summer sweater. It would be cooler in New York than here.

Mom popped her head in as I dragged my bags onto my bed. "It's not pretty, getting in after midnight, and has a four-hour layover in Atlanta, but I have you a flight in about three hours. We have to drive to Austin for it."

I glanced at the clock. We needed to leave within the hour to get to Austin and have time for me to check in. "That's fine, Mom. Thank you."

"I'll pull together what you have out here," she said. "Give me a bag."

I passed her the smaller suitcase and turned to start filling the big one. I saw the picture of me and Quinn and forced myself not to tear it into pieces. That was the past. A good past. But past.

I took it out and stuck it in the corner of my mirror instead. It could stay here with the rest of my history.

Then I concentrated on the work, making sure I didn't miss anything important.

The front door opened and closed. I heard the murmur of voices. I paused. Who was here? My heart leaped that it might be Bennett.

But when a shadow crossed my doorway, it wasn't him.

Quinn.

I clutched the edge of my suitcase, my knees shaking. "What are you doing here?" I asked him.

"I couldn't leave things like that," he said. "I just couldn't."

He moved closer. He had showered and dressed, like he was going for a ride, in jeans and a light T-shirt. Maybe he thought he could get me out on the trail. Fat chance.

"We already said everything." I picked up the last shirt and set it on the stack in the suitcase. "I get you now. I get you in a way I never did before."

Quinn paused by the end of the bed. "Are you leaving? I thought we could take a ride together now that the rain has stopped. Figure this out."

"No," I said. "I have to go."

His face looked stricken. "I know going with Bennett's fiancée was a dick move. I know it. I always want what's in front of me, whoever she is. But that was before you came back."

I didn't buy it. I shoved another leotard in the bag. "Quinn, you're hopeless. I came here to figure out if I could live without you, and I've figured it out. I can."

He took a step toward me, but I didn't turn. Another dance outfit went into the suitcase.

"Juliet. If I lose you, it will be the greatest heartache of my life. The only heartache I've ever known."

I held a pale pink skirt in my hands, so similar to

the ones I wore as a little girl, first trying out my dance. I wasn't her anymore. I understood things now. I set the wisp of fabric on top of the clothes in the bag and turned to him.

"Quinn, a friend can't break your heart."

"But you're breaking mine."

I closed the top of the suitcase. I wasn't angry with Quinn. He couldn't see for himself what was going on.

"You're still a kid, Quinn, just with older play-mates," I said. "I saw you with all those other girls. And you treated me differently. It just wasn't there."

"But that's it," he insisted. "You're different from all those other girls."

I hesitated. Maybe I hadn't been patient. Maybe it would have come with time. But he'd been so inter-ested before he left. The niggle of doubt I'd felt the day he came back became a rush.

"Is this because of Margie?"

He stood up straight. "What about Margie?"

"You acted one way before you left. And another when you came back."

His mouth opened and closed but he didn't say anything.

And this told me what I needed to know. He couldn't deny it. She had been important to him before. And they'd rekindled something.

"I have to go. I honestly hope you figure things out." I dragged the bag off the mattress and headed out of the room.

Mom stood at the front door with my other bag. "You okay?" she asked.

"I have to be," I said. I took the other bag from her.

"I called Adams to help," she said. "It's a long way to walk with bags."

"I did it when I got here," I said. "I can do it now."

She kissed my forehead. "Then let's go." She took one more glance back at my bedroom and shook her head.

We left her little house, heading down the wet path to the stable where staff members parked their cars.

As we walked along the wall, I glanced up at the mansion. I wasn't sure exactly where Bennett's rooms were, but I assumed they were near Quinn's. He was in there somewhere.

Mom saw me looking. "You sure you don't want to go talk to him before you go?" she asked.

"I've had enough dramatic confrontations for one day," I told her.

We loaded my bags in her backseat.

As we drove around the walls to the circle drive

out front, I tried not to look at the estate. I wanted to keep my eyes focused straight ahead. To my future. Not my past. If I'd learned anything in this time at home, it was this:

My past was done.

Chapter Twenty-Three

❧

Two months later

I LOVED THIS INTERPRETATION OF THE FINAL DANCE of *La Traviata*, and not just because I got to be in it.

The story was very centered on the main characters, the courtesan Violetta and her lover Alfredo. Many of the scenes had only two or three characters, including the famous ending.

But our dance company put a new spin on that last scene. Instead of focusing on the tragic lovers, our version included all the characters — the meddling father, the rival lover, the maid, and me as Flora. We all appeared as spirits to anguish over the tragic conclusion.

Each of us had our own guilt and grief to express.

As Violetta's friend, I would circle her lifeless body near the end.

It was a good role. I turned and spun, bits of white floating around me from the ethereal costume made of scarves.

Then I held my final position. The dancer who played Alfredo lifted the limp Violetta up onto his shoulder, attempting to recreate their happy lovers' dance of just a moment ago, then collapsed to the ground, knowing it was over.

The lights went down and the applause began.

I tried not to breathe too hard, maintaining my pose until the curtain was completely closed. Then we scurried off the stage so the chorus dancers could go out for the first bow.

Mom was here for the opening. She had arrived during the last few days of my break and stayed on through rehearsals. She took a leave of absence from the estate. We holed up in my tiny room in Chelsea like school chums. She wandered the practice rooms during the day, getting permission from the trainers to warm up with the other dancers, and had a ball watching everything from fittings to choreography sessions.

It was good for her, and I could tell she was learning a lot, turning over in her mind what might be next for her in her own career. She seemed to sense I was reluctant to return to the estate, so maybe it was time for her to move on as well.

The chorus parted and I ran forward with some of the other minor characters for our ovation. Then we stepped aside for the baron and the father. Then Violetta and Alfredo.

The production would run here for several weeks, then move to Paris for several more.

I was happy. It was a good life.

The curtain came down for the last time and we all hurried offstage to the dressing room. There was nothing so glamorous as individual suites for the dancers. All of us, including Amy, who played the lead role, were dumped into a large room lined with lighted mirrors and chairs, bursting with costume racks and discarded shoes and ribbons.

In the hallway leading to the dressing area, friends and family of the dancers began to filter in from the performance hall. I looked around for my mother. She had connived her way into front-row seats through the cute boy at the box office even though the opening had been sold out for some time. There were always reserves that were let go for patrons who didn't end up attending.

I pushed through the throng. If I didn't spot her quickly, I would just head to the dressing room to get this costume put away and find her afterward. I dodged a tall stout man and peered down the rest of the hall.

And saw him.

Bennett.

My heart stopped. I sucked in a breath. He was here.

A woman was with him, beautiful with dark brown hair. He guided her by the elbow. My stomach turned over. How dare he bring someone with him to my show?

My evening was destroyed. I seethed with jealousy and anger.

Sonbitch Bennett indeed. I wanted to punch him.

Then I spotted Mom. She was with him!

I spun on my heel to get away as fast as I could. But Mom must have seen me. "Juliet! Wait!" she called out.

I was stuck.

I turned and waited for them to arrive. As they approached, I could see the woman was older than I thought.

I forced myself not to look at Bennett. I was already flashing to that last day on his sofa. My face blazed hot.

Mom took my hand. "Juliet, your performance was simply perfection." She gestured to the couple.

"I'm sure you remember Bennett. This is his mother, Carrie."

My jaw dropped. "His mother?"

The woman extended a hand. "Lovely to meet you. I understand you had a hand in convincing Bennett to contact me. I owe you a debt of gratitude."

"I—I did?" I stammered. "You do?"

I couldn't look at Bennett. In the two months since I left the Claremont estate, my thoughts had turned to him often. Sometimes I pined. Most times I burned with anger and embarrassment that I'd been played so hard. A token in his revenge plot.

"I do," Carrie said. "We've had two lovely visits, one in Portland, where I live now, and then this one here in New York." She glanced around the halls, which were starting to quiet down as people met up and moved on with their evenings. "It's very exciting back here." She gazed down at me. "You were very lovely to watch. I can see why Bennett is taken with you."

Now I couldn't help but snap my head around to look at him. He stood stock still, hard as granite, like that night at the suite when he hadn't wanted to talk about his mother. He nodded almost imperceptibly at me.

"We'd love to take you to dinner," Carrie said. "Right, Bennett?"

She looked over at him, but he had barely moved, frozen in place.

He didn't want that. He had no more use for me.

I sent a pleading look at my mother. She could not do this!

Mom totally got it. "Juliet is looking a little more peaked than usual from this performance and she has a matinée tomorrow," she said. "Can we take a rain check on that?"

"Of course," Carrie said. "I really did love the show."

"Thank you," I said.

Bennett still hadn't spoken, but he nodded at me again as they turned away.

Mom walked with me back to the dressing room.

"I'm so sorry, Juliet. Bennett contacted me yesterday asking if it would be okay to bring his mother to your show."

I pushed through the dressing room door, stripping off parts of my costume as I went. I didn't have anything to say.

I picked up a soft blue T-shirt and jerked it over my head, then pulled my bodice off underneath it. Thankfully, this production didn't have any required appearances afterward, just a cast party I could safely skip. I was not up for socializing.

"Are we still doing our traditional night at the Hyatt?" Mom asked.

I wrapped myself in a skirt so I could jerk the tights off and replaced my toe shoes with sandals. "Of course. I just didn't expect to see him."

Mother sat on the stool next to me. "You sure things are done between you two?" she asked.

"We haven't even talked in two months. He didn't even try." I handed the wispy scarves and bodice to a costume assistant who was organizing the racks.

"Neither did you."

"I wasn't the one acting like an ass."

I retrieved the bag she carried for me and shoved my tights and toe shoes inside. We meandered through the room to the back exit. The Hyatt was only a few city blocks down. And it was our tradition.

Thankfully nowhere on our walk was Sonbitch Bennett.

Chapter Twenty-Four

When we got to our rooms, Mom came over so we could order our usual late-night room service. While we pored over the menu, she got three texts in a row but ignored them.

"Who is that?" I asked.

She shrugged. "Probably Carrie. I was supposed to sneak off with her if things went well with you and Bennett."

"Mom!"

"Well? We thought you'd fall into each other's arms. We were wrong." She picked up her phone and scrolled through the texts.

"What does she want?"

She read for a second, then said, "Bennett didn't want to go out, and she's asking where she can grab a meal without feeling awkward about being alone in the city."

Guilt stabbed me. "Why don't you go with her?" I said. "It sounds like you hit it off."

"I like her a lot. I did while she was Mrs. Claremont number three. I hated what happened to her after Bennett was born."

I fell back on the bed. "I could probably stand to just go to sleep," I said. "This time isn't like the other opening nights, where you were only here a couple days. You've been here for weeks."

She laughed. "I may be overstaying my welcome."

I draped my arm over my face. "No, no. It's not that. And it's fine for you to go rescue Carrie. We can go out any night. I think I need to recover from seeing Bennett anyway."

She sat next to me. "Don't you think that if it upsets you this much, there is something there?"

"Sure there is. Animosity and disbelief," I said. I moved my arm so I could see her. "Seriously, Mom. Go save Carrie."

She stood up. "Okay. She's not far. You text me if you need me."

"I will." I closed my eyes. I wanted some time alone. The image of Bennett standing among all those people in that perfect suit was burned into me.

I wanted to sleep it off, like a bad drug. Or a hangover.

Mom kissed my forehead and slipped out the door. In the quiet of the room, I started to calm down. I wanted the Claremonts behind me. I might not ever get over Bennett, any more than I had gotten over Quinn as a girl, but I could still move forward.

There was a quiet knock at the door. We hadn't actually ordered any food, so Mom must have forgotten something.

I forced myself up.

But when I opened the door, nobody was there.

On the floor was a silver box.

I wondered if Mom had left it for me. I glanced both ways down the hall. Empty.

I kept the door propped open as I lifted the lid.

Inside was a note.

"You really were saying good-bye that day. A ballerina should have both her slippers."

Beneath it was the match of the shoe Bennett gave me the night of the party. The one we were supposed to give a proper fitting.

The elevator dinged. Bennett!

I didn't even think about how angry I was or what had happened between us. I just knew he had come back a second time, and maybe I owed him the chance to talk. I could do that much. Listen.

I snatched the slipper and set the box on the ground to prop open the door. Then I ran down the hall and around the corner, hoping to stop him from leaving.

The elevator was still open, but inside was only an elderly lady who looked at me quizzically. "Going down?" she asked.

I shook my head and backed away. He was just here. Where had he gone?

We were on the tenth floor. I made a mad dash down the hall for the nearest stairwell.

I flung open the door and began descending in a panic.

When I got to the first landing, I peered down.

And saw a suited arm with a hand holding the railing.

"Bennett?"

The movement stopped and he leaned into the space to look up.

I kept going down. "Bennett!"

He waited for me, less granite now, managing a small smile. "Juliet."

I paused a few stairs above him. I held out the slipper. "You can't just leave it. You were supposed to try it on me." I hesitated, not sure if I should say the next part. But I did. "We should at least find out if it's the right fit."

He had to clear his throat before he said, "Is that an invitation?"

I nodded and turned to go back up the stairs. He followed, catching up in time to open the exit door.

Our steps were whisper soft on the carpet as we returned to my room.

"Clever," he said, bending to retrieve the box.

"I didn't have an elevator opening directly to my Presidential Suite," I said. "You're seriously slumming it to be in a mid-hallway room with a view of an alley."

The door closed behind us as we moved inside. I sat on the edge of the bed, the shoe in my lap. Now that we were here, I felt less certain about what would happen next. After a long silence I asked, "Bennett, why did you come? It's been two months."

He stood a safe distance from me. "I know what Quinn said to you. That I was just getting back at him. Revenge for Pamela."

"Were you?"

He paused. "I was the one who tipped off the photographers."

My head pounded. "So you were just trying to get even."

"He was pretty taken with you," he said. "But I did want to save you the sorrow. That was part of it."

My anger threatened to spill out, scathing and hot, but I kept it in check. "And what was the rest?"

"You," he said. "You came onto the estate like a breath of fresh air."

I didn't buy it. "You hurt me."

"I didn't think that was possible. You were in love with Quinn," he said.

"No, Bennett," I retorted. "I was in love with you." I clapped my hand over my mouth. Why had I just said that?

God. I hadn't even said it to myself.

Bennett moved forward then, carefully, slowly, as if I might startle away. And he knelt in front of me and held out his hand for the slipper.

I passed it to him, still shocked at myself for what I had said. My eyes pricked with emotion. I had never felt this painful combination of exhilaration and misery with his brother Quinn. It was true that I had wanted to be around Quinn. And I had not been happy after I had gone away.

But Bennett was an entirely different order of magnitude. I just hadn't recognized it for what it was.

Bennett eased my sandal off my foot, taking a moment to cup his hands over the bruised, reddened toes from my long day of rehearsals and a performance.

"Ballerinas' feet aren't pretty when they aren't in their shoes," I managed to get out.

He bent to press a kiss on my bare ankle. "It just shows the hard work it takes to appear so beautiful and effortless."

The shoe glittered as he slid it over my foot. My heel rested perfectly against the back. It fit. Of course it did. Bennett would have had it no other way.

"I don't have the match for it here," I said.

"Isn't that it?" he asked, gesturing at the chair where I had set down the bag Mom had carried. Beside it rested the other silver slipper.

Oh, Mom. She'd been in on this all along.

Bennett took the three strides to the chair and retrieved the shoe.

The second one fit just as perfectly.

I lifted my legs to admire the pair. "They are exquisite," I said.

He sat beside me on the bed. "So is your dance."

My eyes wouldn't quite lift to his face. I felt exposed after what I had said to him. But he was here.

"Do you remember that night in the stables, the night you left for New York?" he asked.

I nodded.

"You told your horse that you loved Quinn and you always would."

I had nothing to say to that. I ran my fingers along the swirl pattern on the bedspread. I felt small on the big bed.

"I thought about that night all the time," Bennett said. "That innocent but powerful pronouncement. How you believed it with all your heart."

I could see the details of his suit jacket, the handkerchief folded neatly in his breast pocket. The gleaming buttons. I still couldn't look into his face.

"And from then on, I judged every girl I met by the measuring stick of you."

My head snapped up at that. I had done the same thing. But with Quinn!

"And even when I asked Pamela to marry me, I knew somehow this wasn't it. She didn't feel the way you felt about Quinn. And neither did I. So what Quinn told you was probably true. I wasn't enough. I reserved the most important part of myself and kept it from her."

He was so close that I could turn my face and kiss him. And I almost did, wanting to erase the pain he must have felt after realizing he'd made a mistake and that he was going to hurt someone.

But I didn't have to. Bennett was already there

and brushed his lips against mine, gently, as if he was just trying to see if it were okay.

I relaxed into him, my body resting against his shoulder. He kept the kiss easy and light, although one hand came to touch my jaw.

After a moment, I pulled back. I had to know where he was with this, what had brought him here.

"What about now?" I asked. "Where is the most important part of yourself?"

He picked up my hand and pressed it with his against my chest. "It's all right here."

This time I leaned into him first, and there was no gentleness to this kiss. It was more than a meeting of our lips, but a collision of need.

His mouth sought mine, hungry, devouring.

I wanted closer to him, so close. During a dance, my body was often tucked against my partner, and often we moved like we were one person. I wanted this with Bennett. To be that incredibly together.

He pulled me up against him and I turned to face him on his lap, my legs wrapped around his waist.

I tugged at his stiff jacket, pushing it off his shoulders and tossing it away.

His shirt was soft and silky, so well made. I ran my hands along it, my skin humming with the touch of the smooth fabric.

I unbuttoned it with speed and agility. Despite all

that had happened in his office that day, I had seen nothing of him.

I wanted to discover him.

He also wore a thin white shirt, too fine to be cotton. I felt the muscles of his chest beneath the coolness of it, but impatiently grasped the bottom and pulled it over his head.

Now I had his skin. I could not stop touching him, the bulging shoulders, the corded neck, the ripple of his abs.

When I reached for his belt, he broke the kiss, his breath ragged. No longer content to let me do all the work, he twisted us around until I was on my back on the bed. Before I realized what was happening, the wraparound skirt was gone and my shirt had flown across the room.

I was down to panties and the silver slippers.

Bennett moved over me, his hands and mouth everywhere, branding my skin. I arched my back as he brought a breast to his tongue. I could think of nothing, nothing but the need and pleasure sparking through me like an electric current.

"I have thought of this every day since I last saw you," he said, his voice low. "I'm going to do everything that's tortured me."

He jerked my panties down. His fingers slid between my thighs and his mouth soon followed, anguished, determined, hot.

I lunged upward on the bed, increasing the pressure, my hands in his hair. I was so lost. I could barely breathe.

He pushed me up just like he had before, expertly drawing me into the passion he was feeling, until I couldn't take it anymore.

"Bennett, please," I begged.

He withdrew only his hand, still nipping at me with his mouth. I heard his shoes fall off the edge of the bed, and his pants slid to the floor with a jingle.

Then he was over me, face next to mine. "Condom?" he asked.

"Pill," I said.

And he was inside me, splitting me wide so hard and fast that I cried out.

He braced on one elbow, his other hand on my cheek, watching me. "I want to hear you again," he said. "I've heard that sound over and over again in my dreams."

I held on to his waist, the rapid motion of him over me making the world tilt. He reached between us, teasing the nub as he worked, and there was no holding anything back. I called for him as the orgasm rocked me, tears coming down, the world exploding.

Bennett slid his arm beneath me and held me tightly against him. His body rocked into mine, pressing more deeply, moving with me more perfectly than any dance. Then he groaned next to my ear and held still, flooding me with warmth and wet.

I clutched at him, breathing hard, trying to right my vision and find the ground again.

My braids were tumbling down, and Bennett released the pins, then laid me back on the bed. He fell beside me and I turned to curl into him.

We stayed that way a while, letting our breathing slow. Outside our room, doors opened and closed. The elevator dinged. The world intruded.

"I see why you buy out entire floors," I said finally.

He laughed. "You want me to take over this one?"

I pushed on his chest. "And kick out all the neighbors we just annoyed?"

He pulled me close. "Let them be annoyed."

I lifted a leg to show off my silver shoes. "I just had sex with slippers on."

"That's one way to break them in," Bennett said.

I snuggled into his neck. "How did this happen?" I asked.

His voice was low and heavy with emotion. "It was so damn hard watching you dance up there. I wanted to join you onstage. I wanted to be the one to hold your hand and turn you in a circle."

I remembered our dance in my mother's studio.

How I had fulfilled his wish. It had been a perfect moment. There weren't many perfect moments in the world.

I sat up. "So why don't you, then?"

I stood and tugged on his arms until he was up with me. We were naked, other than my shoes. And we had no music. There was no beat, no rhythm, no sounds to guide us.

But when Bennett took his first step on the soft carpet of the hotel room, I knew exactly how my movements would fit against his.

And we danced. Silent other than the whisper of our feet and the gentle rush of our breath.

A waltz. And as we moved, I knew which one ran through both our heads, how we fit so perfectly together. The "Dreamcatcher Waltz." And if fate had put us exactly where I knew it should, the music that led us would never, ever fade.

Epilogue

࿊

Four months later

WHEN BENNETT AND I PULLED UP BEFORE THE NEW
dance academy, Mom stood in front of the double
doors with the biggest smile I'd ever seen. With
several months of growth, her hair had that edgy
Annie Lennox look, especially since she'd tipped the
edges with blue. She could easily pass for thirty.

A smattering of photographers waited on the
sidewalk. Normally I wouldn't have expected
coverage of the opening of a small business like this,
but the Claremont name always garnered attention.

Plus, there was the charity angle. Bennett had
divided a portion of the estate for the first Claremont
baby, who had survived only seven minutes after his

birth. He created a fund that would support the functions of the academy that provided free dance lessons for children in families affected by cancer. Mom was going to handle those classes herself.

"We should probably get out there," Bennett said.

I opened the door. Mom spotted me and waved. When the photographers realized Bennett was here, they trained their cameras our way. He didn't smile or address them like Quinn would have, but put his arm around my waist and led us to the base of the steps.

I thought about the footage I'd seen of Quinn before I shut off my Google alert on his name, leading Margie to the premiere of one of her movies. They were engaged again, and I was glad. He'd realized something on that trip to California, just like I guessed. I wasn't his heartbreak after all.

"Are you coming up here?" Mom called.

"This is your spotlight," Bennett said.

A muscled dark-skinned man in a black silk shirt and slim pants handed Mom an oversized pair of scissors to cut the ribbon tied across the doors. This must be Jacob, the first instructor Mom had hired. He was a dancer who specialized in jazz. I looked forward to meeting him.

Another dancer in a pink leotard and long sheer skirt waited on the side to pull the banner that would reveal the name of the studio. Mom had kept this bit of information even from me, but said Bennett had been in on it.

Mom snapped the wide pink ribbon and it fell to the ground.

The girl in pink released the banner and it fluttered to one side.

My breath caught as I read the name.

Dreamcatcher Dance Academy.

The waltz I first danced with Bennett.

I squeezed his hand. "I love it," I whispered.

Flashes popped. Mom waved everyone inside and disappeared through the doors.

"Let's let them all get through," Bennett said.

We hesitated on the bottom step, letting the reporters and Mom's dance friends push ahead. A woman in an electric wheelchair rolled up the ramp on the right side.

After a moment, the front was quiet.

We climbed the steps slowly. The bright white words on the stone façade overhead warmed my heart. Dreamcatcher. We would never forget that moment now.

By the time we got inside the foyer, Mom and the small crowd had moved on to one of the studios. The dancer who had dropped the banner sat behind a big round counter where students would one day check in.

"They've all gone into the Claremont Memorial Studio if you'd like to catch up," she said cheerily.

"Which one is last on their agenda?" Bennett asked.

"I think Danika planned to save the Dance of the Shades Room for last, since it has the wraparound image of her daughter in the production."

"This is Danika's daughter," Bennett said.

"Oh!" The girl stood up. "I didn't recognize you with your hair down!"

"That's okay. I'm not exactly Julia Roberts or anything," I said.

"You are around here!" The girl's face flushed. "Do you want me to take you to your mom?"

"We're fine," Bennett said. "We'll find our way."

The girl sat down, her face still as pink as her outfit.

We walked down a hallway. Through the window, we could see Mom talking to the crowd in the first room.

"It's a two-way mirror," Bennett said. "They can't see us." He led us farther down the corridor. Each wall held two studios with a bench outside the door, and another one inside along the wall, so parents could watch from either place.

"It's nice," I said.

"Danika got it just the way she wanted it," Bennett said.

We approached the last studio on the opposite side. Above the door read "Studio 4: Dance of the Shades."

Bennett turned the handle and gestured for me to go inside.

One wall was all mirrors behind a barre. In one corner was a small rectangular bump-out with two doors. Storage, I assumed. And maybe a bathroom. Then the wall with the mirrored window and the bench.

The fourth wall was entirely covered with a gigantic image from *La Bayadère*. We were about one-third of the way through the Shades dance, where a number of dancers were already out, but squarely in the center of the image was me. We were all at the height of the arabesque, absolutely in sync, with perfect execution of the leg lift.

"Wow," I said.

"If that isn't inspiring, I don't know what is," Bennett said.

But when I turned to him, he wasn't looking at the images.

He was looking at me.

My throat tightened. "This is an amazing space,

Bennett. I'm so happy it's been built. What a wonderful thing for my mother to be involved in."

"It's hers," he said. "I'll have my business manager check in with her every once in a while if she needs advice on the financial end."

"Good idea," I said. "She's never run anything like it."

"She'll have help."

Bennett squeezed my hand and let go.

I tilted my head. "You seem nervous. Do you hate reporters?"

He drew in a deep breath. "I do, but..."

His hand dipped into his suit jacket pocket. When he drew it out, he held a small black velvet box.

Then he got down on one knee.

My breath caught. "Bennett?"

He looked up at me, his face as uncertain as I'd ever seen it, a far cry from the Bennett who brokered business deals and dominated boardrooms.

The door to the studio opened and noise filled the room as Mom and the entire entourage flooded inside.

"Oh!" Mom said. "I didn't realize!"

She moved as if she'd shepherd everyone out, but she was way too late. Bennett was down on one knee, holding the ring box open, and those cameras started popping like mad.

"So much for this being the last stop," I said to Bennett. "We have an audience!"

"I guess you're used to performing in front of people," he said.

I laughed. "That I am."

The reporters started shushing one another so they could hear.

"Have you asked her yet?" one called out. My mother smacked him on the arm.

"I was just waiting for you all," Bennett said easily, and the room relaxed.

A couple dozen people crowded inside. Probably there were more in the hall on the other side of the mirrored window.

Mom waited expectantly, her face glowing, her hands clasped under her chin.

Bennett looked up at me. "Juliet Small, ballerina extraordinaire, strong, amazing woman, and love of my life, will you marry me?"

The ring winked at me from the cushion inside the box. My gaze moved from it to Bennett's earnest face.

"Yes," I said. "As long as you promise always to dance."

"I do," he said.

The spectators cheered. Bennett placed the ring on my finger and stood. He twirled me in a gentle circle that drew me into his body as the flashes fired nonstop.

And when he kissed me, I knew we had both found our way, beyond the hang-ups that had driven our past and the starry-eyed youthfulness that had kept us from seeing what was right before us all along.

And I knew our dance would never, ever end.

I hope you enjoyed *The Billionaire's Dance!* It is a standalone, but the Dreamcatcher Dance Studio that Bennett builds for Juliet's mother becomes the setting for the Lovers Dance series that starts with Forbidden Dance. You will see Bennett and Juliet again in that story — they are an important element in bringing together the next pair of dancers!

Also by Deanna Roy

The Forever Series

A young couple reunites in colleges, four years after the death of their newborn.

Book one Forever Innocent *is FREE on all venues.*

- Forever Innocent (Corabelle & Gavin)
- Forever Loved (Corabelle & Gavin)
- Forever Sheltered (Tina & Darion)
- Forever Bound (Jenny & Chance)
- Forever Family (Corabelle, Tina, Jenny)
- Forever Christmas (Corabelle & Gavin)

- Boxed Set: First Three Books
- Boxed Set: Final Three Books

- Stella and Dane (Standalone)

The Lovers Dance Series

SWOONY DANCE ROMANCE

A sheltered ballerina is lured into the life of a brash TV reality show star.

- Forbidden Dance
- Wounded Dance
- Wicked Dance
- Tender Dance
- Final Dance

- Lovers Dance Boxed Set

- Billionaire's Dance (a standalone prequel)

Other Books

- Conversations with Little Dude (Nonfiction stories with her son who was adopted from foster care)
- In the Company of Angels (A fill-in-the-pages baby record book for babies lost to miscarriage or stillbirth)
- The Magic Mayhem trilogy of action/adventure books for children ages 9-12.

If you prefer your romances with no graphic love scenes or coarse language

You will love Deanna's pen name Abby Tyler. As Abby, Deanna writes funny, feel-good small-town romances with

a recurring cast of feisty senior citizens and the couples they push together, by hook or by crook.

 **Deanna** is the six-time *USA Today* bestselling author of romance and women's fiction.

She is a passionate advocate for women who have miscarried. She founded the web site Pregnancy-Loss.info in 1998 after the loss of her first baby and continues to run both online and in-person support groups for women who have endured this impossible loss.

She is a foster mom, an adoptive mom, and a baby loss mom. She lives in Austin, Texas, with her family.

Learn more about the author at
www.deannaroy.com

Join her email or text list for new release notices at
Deanna's List

f facebook.com/deannaroyauthor

🐦 twitter.com/deannaroy

📷 instagram.com/deannaroyauthor

g goodreads.com/Goodreads

BB bookbub.com/authors/deanna-roy